The Lady in White

Book Three

Ghosts of Summerleigh Series

By M.L. Bullock

Dedication

For Jeopardy Belle.

Oh, lady bright! can it be right—
This window open to the night?
The wanton airs, from the tree-top,
Laughingly through the lattice drop—
The bodiless airs, a wizard rout,
Flit through thy chamber in and out,
And wave the curtain canopy

Excerpt from *The Sleeper*

Edgar Allan Poe, 1831

Prologue—Harper Belle

Desire, Mississippi
November 1948

"Addison Lee, you look like a princess! A real princess." Loxley squealed beside me and clapped her hands before she raced to hug our trembling sister. Loxley was right. Addie did look like a princess, a nervous one with a handful of shedding buttercups, quivering lips and a worrisomely pale face. It was so like Addison to get a case of the jitters on her wedding day—had I expected anything less? Poor Addie had a lifelong relationship with her distraught nerves, but she never wavered in her determination to marry Frank Harlow. And for that, she had my utmost respect. In fact, if I were to be really honest with myself, I would have to admit that Addison was braver than I. The idea of leaving Summerleigh, of leaving Aunt Dot and the others behind, was too much to bear.

Addison was as beautiful as any of those girls in the magazines that we used to spend hours admiring. My younger sister surprised us with her wedding dress choice, a tea-length, scoop-necked, short-sleeved gown. But as it was an afternoon wedding, it seemed appropriate. Although I was no fan of the coral-colored bridesmaid dresses we'd been asked to wear, I felt stylish and pretty. And for sweet Addison Lee, I would wear chicken wire if I had to.

Just this morning, Aunt Dot surprised Addie with a pearl choker that now shook around her thin neck while Loxley and I gifted her with a pair of glistening hair combs. The four of us had a tearful moment then, but Aunt Dot never mentioned Momma. She didn't say how proud Momma would be of Addison or how much Momma must wish she could have made the trip, and I was thankful for that. We never talked about poor, crazy Momma locked away in the asylum far from Summerleigh. No. We never talked about her, and I did my best not to think of her. *Stop that, Harper. This is a happy day.* There were enough shadows here at Summerleigh without adding one more, especially today. After dabbing at her eyes with an embroidered handkerchief, Aunt Dot scurried out of Addison's bedroom, presumably to direct the caterers and waitstaff and even early guests who had begun to arrive at Summerleigh. The old house would be alive again today, at least for a little while. Aunt Dot had managed to turn the place into a comfortable home for us, but it had its cold spots. Its empty places.

The three of us were alone now; it was just us Belle girls. This was the first time we'd been alone in so very long. I could tell by my sisters' expressions that they were aware of the moment too and that they also felt the shadows of the ones who hadn't made it to witness this glorious day. None of us mentioned Jeopardy or Daddy, and we didn't have to. Addison's lip began to tremble, but I prevented her from speaking a sad word with a squeeze of my hand. I refused to allow the Belle melancholy to settle over us and intrude on this wonderful day.

"Addison Lee, you look every bit a dream. Frank Harlow is a lucky man. But never forget, even when you change your name, you will always be a Belle—and that means something special. To Loxley and to me." Loxley nodded and smiled broadly beside me.

"I will not forget that, Harper. I could never forget my sisters, and I won't be far away. You can visit me anytime you like, both of you. In fact, I insist on it. Promise me? Promise you will come next week for tea or for lunch?"

Loxley and I hugged her, and I clung to them so tightly it surprised me. How could I let either of them go when it had been my job to take care of them? I'd been doing it for so long. Just like Daddy would have wanted—and like Momma always expected me to. But Addison loved her Frank, and he most assuredly loved her.

Tall, skinny Frank with his horn-rimmed glasses and slight overbite. He owned a gas station in Lucedale and perpetually smelled of gasoline, but he was a nice enough young man. I wasn't surprised that he asked Addison to marry him, since he had been crazy for her for a long time, but I was glad that Aunt Dot had insisted that Addison graduate high school first. I think Addison was glad too. Now the only one left in school was Loxley.

I had been out for two years now but still hadn't left for college. For some reason, I dithered. I hesitated. In the back of my mind, I told myself that it was responsibility that slowed me down. *How could I leave Loxley and Addison without safely depositing them into their futures?* But that wasn't the truth. I hid myself away here at Summerleigh for entirely selfish reasons.

Because I didn't want to face a world without Jeopardy Belle in it.

And if I stayed here, I would never have to think about Ben's secret. I wouldn't be tempted to tell anyone. I could never do that.

As we hugged, I pretended Jeopardy was with us too, that she was holding us and smiling, her wild hair in an unruly cloud around her face. Maybe she was. I didn't see ghosts on a regular basis, not like Loxley, but I imagined Jeopardy hovering near us now as I often did. What silly thing would she say if she were here? What words of advice would she want to impart to Addison? I struggled for the appropriate words, the right encouragement to share with Addie, but I could think of nothing. Nothing that wouldn't make us all weepy at the prospect of being separated forever. And we would be. No matter what Addison said or how we all pretended otherwise, we would be separated forever. Marriage was a forever thing.

A tap on the bedroom door broke the spell of that poignant moment, and we fell back laughing and wiping away the odd tear. Mr. Foshee, the photographer, had arrived and wasted no time in ordering us about. Addison's small room had been beautifully decorated for the bridal photo shoot, but we were taking some photos outside too. That was worrisome, as it promised to be warmer than any of us had expected. November was normally much cooler than this, but I wouldn't complain. I would sweat and smile and be happy for Addison. Today would be perfect for her. It had to be.

I think I was the first one to hear the footsteps overhead. The photographer reminded me to smile, and Loxley glanced in my direction, her eyes immediately rising to the ceiling above us. My eyes met hers as Addie smiled and fluffed her dress on the settee. She clutched my hand, and I remembered to smile at the camera.

There it was again, clear as a bell. Footsteps. But not heavy footfalls, the sounds of high heels, a lady's footsteps. And I could see that Addison heard them too.

I said, "It's probably a guest, Addie. Someone's up there exploring is all." Loxley began to shake her head as if she disagreed with me, but I frowned at her in an attempt to remind her that we should think of Addison.

Ignore the ghosts, Loxley. Ignore them all.

I knew she couldn't hear me, but I couldn't bring myself to say the words aloud. Thankfully, Mr. Foshee decided that it was time to go outside and take our outdoor photos. He glanced at his watch and reminded us that we would have to hurry. We didn't want to bring bad luck on the bride by letting the bridegroom see her before the wedding. We followed Mr. Foshee out of Summerleigh, but of course we were stopped numerous times along the way as everyone wanted to congratulate Addison.

With just minutes to spare before we had to spirit her away, we gathered beneath the large oak tree in the backyard. Fall leaves were everywhere, and it was a beautiful setting for a wedding photo. I couldn't help but smile at Addison's beautiful face lit with happiness at long last. Mr. Foshee snapped his fingers and reminded us all to watch him as he took the final photo. The light popped, and we all froze for a moment, laughing and smiling.

Everyone except me.

All I could do was stare at the girl who watched us from the attic window. She didn't move or try to hide from me. She didn't vanish as you would expect a spirit to do. This wasn't Jeopardy watching us from on high.

The pale face, even paler than Addison's, peered back at me, her expression sad and empty. Her eyes met mine, and I knew she wanted me to see her. She wanted me to know that she was there, that she watched us. And I knew who she was.

She was the Lady in White.

Chapter One—Jerica Poole

I woke to the sounds of a circular saw whirring. Obviously, Jesse was trying to get a jump on the crown molding that we were scheduled to install today, but I really wanted to sleep. No such luck since the guest room overlooked his garage where he was hard at work. I groaned and pushed my hair out of my face. The clock said nine, but it felt much earlier than that. *Too early, Jesse.*

I wanted to—no, I needed to sleep. Between the late nights we'd spent planning the renovation, my regular bouts of sleeplessness and my romantic interludes with Jesse, I felt like I'd never catch up on my rest. It was as if my biorhythmic schedule was completely out of whack. I felt drained and a bit cranky as I tossed around for one last minute before getting up to greet the day. For the first time, I didn't feel like bounding down the stairs and kissing him on the cheek. There would be no lighthearted chatter as we ran boards, taped them and loaded them on the truck. This morning, despite having genuine romantic feelings for him, I dreaded facing Jesse.

Why in the world would he ask me to marry him now? I told myself that it wasn't that he asked but how he did it that bothered me, but I couldn't be sure. Yes, Jesse Clarke was an amazing man. A skilled carpenter, a good friend and a talented lover. Yes, we were great together, but I guess I just didn't see it coming. I, Jerica Jernigan Poole, was blindsided. Again. And I didn't like it.

"I think Jerica Clarke has a nice ring to it. Just think, we wouldn't even have to fight over mono-grammed towels."

"Tell me you're joking. I'm not the kind of girl who has monogrammed towels."

I'd tried to brush it off, joke about it, but I could see the hurt in his dark eyes. Our conversation moved on, and so did our lovemaking, but that halfhearted proposal hung between us like a living thing.

It's time to go home, Jerica. And that's what I planned to do. I wasn't mad at Jesse, at least I didn't think I was, but we needed to put some space between us. I mean, it wouldn't be a long space since we had work to do together, but at least I could have a few minutes to myself. I slid on my jeans and t-shirt and searched for my shoes. How was it that I, a grown woman, could lose my shoes so easily? I was worse than a child. I kicked them off wherever I landed and never remembered to put them in my closet.

And then I recalled last night's dream.

I dreamed of Harper and Addison and of course sweet Loxley; it had been so long since I'd seen them, at least a full six months. They were so happy and full of life, but the dream hadn't really been about the Belles. I hadn't been there to see them. It was someone else who wanted to be seen. Like Harper, my attention had been drawn away from Addison and her special day. Away from the coral crepe paper and the candles, away from the heavily frosted cake and the table of carefully wrapped wedding gifts. My attention had been on the ghost in the attic, the young woman we'd all believed was the murdered Mariana McIntyre. And now that I recalled the moment when our eyes locked, I remembered something else.

She spoke to me!

Just a few words; I heard them in my ear, but now as I woke, I couldn't recall them. And that filled me with sadness.

This wasn't the first time I'd thought about the Lady in White this week. Not once but twice I'd walked into the Great Room during our renovation work to find the space filled with an unusual floral scent. No one else seemed to notice the aroma, so I kept my observations to myself. It was certainly a flowery perfume, old and sweet and not one that I recognized. But it had been just as if someone left the room right before me. And that made sense; history had proved that the ghost of Mariana McIntyre liked to avoid the living as much as possible. Now that the Belles were at peace and nobody lived at Summerleigh—not yet, at any rate—the Lady in White was free to roam the house again.

And she was asking for something. Was it help? Yes, she'd spoken to me. My ear remained icy from the encounter. I rubbed at it while I wracked my brain.

I had to get home. I had to go back to Summerleigh.

Chapter Two—Jerica

"Hey, I'm headed back. I'll see you there, okay?"

Jesse pushed his safety glasses up and stared at me questioningly. "I didn't hear you. What's that, Jerica?" He turned the saw off and leaned back on the flipped-down tailgate. "You're leaving?"

I shuffled my feet awkwardly as I slid my hands into my back pockets. I had my overnight bag tossed over my shoulder and apparently forgot to zip it up all the way because some of my underthings fell in the dirt beside me.

Great, Jerica. Perfect timing.

Well, no sense in being embarrassed by the sight of my underwear. It's not like he hadn't already seen me in and out of them. Still, my face flushed as I squatted down and stuffed the dusty items back in my bag.

"Got to get back home. Need to put some laundry in and do a few other things," I lied. "I'll see you at Summerleigh, okay?"

Jesse didn't respond and didn't try to stop me as I walked away and quickly wheeled out of his driveway. As I glanced in my side mirror, I could see his questioning look become one of steely determination. He shook his head, marked another board and made another cut with the saw. I gave him a half-hearted wave, not that he was even looking in my direction, and headed down the street feeling like a Class-A jerk. With a sigh, I turned onto Highway 98 and blazed a trail toward Hurlette Drive. Except for a few turns, it was basically a straight shot back; there was very little traffic and nothing but pastureland for scenery. At least it wasn't a long drive and I wouldn't have to think for too long about what an ass I was being. This was all wrong.

Was I really mad at Jesse because he didn't get down on one knee and propose? What was wrong with me?

I turned down the drive and eased toward the house. Every time I drove up and cleared that last hedge, I caught my breath. Not because of the size of the house or the history it represented but because it was mine. Summerleigh was mine to care for and protect, and the responsibility of it all weighed on me.

I didn't bother pulling around back and parking at the cottage. This was where I was supposed to be, here at the big house. Mariana McIntyre wanted me to come here. She told me something important— why couldn't I remember it? And why did it feel like a matter of life and death? I put the vehicle in park and slid out of the seat. I'd been in such a hurry to get here that I hadn't even turned the air conditioner on, and I was sweating already.

My eyes scanned the newly replaced windows, but there was nothing to see. No ghosts stared back at me as they had in the past. Had I imagined last night's dream? Had I ginned up the urgency I felt to return to Summerleigh just to get out of an awkward conversation with Jesse? I hoped not. I walked up the front steps and slid the key in the door. There was no resistance, and as I stepped inside, no odd sounds. No ladies' heels clunked on the wood above me, but for a fleeting moment I caught a whiff of that strange perfume.

Then nothing.

I walked around the bottom floor for a few minutes, still amazed at everything that had been accomplished in the past six months since Ben Hartley's tragedy. And that's what it had been, a horrible tragedy. There were no more burn marks, no evidence of a deadly conflagration. Everything was new and fresh. I waited, my ears pricked up for any noise. Anything at all.

I whispered, "Harper? Are you here?" Of course, there was no answer. She was gone, at rest now. Right? As I put my foot on the stairs to go check the top floor, my phone rang and I nearly jumped out of my skin. I dug my phone out of my pocket and studied the screen. And that was the last name I expected to see.

"Yes, this is Jerica," I said coldly. Anytime I talked to Detective Michelle Easton, I always got bad news. Why would this call be any different?

"Hi, Jerica. This is Detective Easton. I have an update I thought you should know about. It's about your husband, Eddie. Did I catch you at a bad time?"

"Eddie is my ex-husband, Detective. What kind of update? Did you recover my stolen photos? Some of my property?"

Of course this is a bad time. I never like hearing from you, lady.

"Have you heard from Eddie at all, Jerica? Any calls from him? Have you noticed anything strange lately?"

"No. He doesn't have my phone number. Why are you asking me this?" My skin continued to crawl as the conversation dragged along. I felt an uneasiness growing in the pit of my stomach. I sat on the second step of the staircase and waited for the evasive detective to get to the true reason for her call. She went on and on about procedures and Miranda rights, and I wasn't really sure what she was getting at. "Please bottom-line it for me, Michelle. Do me that kindness, please."

"He's out, Jerica. Eddie is out. We don't know where he is, and I wouldn't be surprised if he's looking for you."

"What do you mean, 'He's out'? Are you telling me that Eddie isn't behind bars where you promised me he'd be? Remember that, Detective? You warned me that because he would be a three-time loser, he'd never get out. And I believed you. What the hell are you people doing?"

Detective Easton's voice was calm and reserved, but she couldn't hide that she was concerned and embarrassed by his untimely release. "Nobody could have predicted that this would happen, Jerica. It's just one of those weird things. A glitch in the system. I'm sorry I didn't catch it sooner, but we're looking for him now. And I expect we will apprehend him before he can make his way out of the state."

"Out of the state? And what do you mean it was a glitch? Somebody let him out on accident?"

Easton sniffed on the other end, and her voice dropped like she was trying to be quiet. "Kind of like that. He made some accusations about his rights not being read properly—it was all bogus, but the judge had to hear his motion. For a poor guy, he has one heck of a swanky lawyer. Eddie was being processed for trial, and someone entered the wrong code. It's as simple and stupid as that. That's not the worst part."

I began to pace the Great Room wondering if I really wanted to know what the "worst part" could be. "And that is?"

"He knows where you are, Jerica. He knows the address. It was on his paperwork. I'm really concerned for your well-being. I think it would be wise for you to go to the sheriff's office there. What is that, George County? Go tell them about this situation. Give them my number so we can coordinate our efforts. I'm sure we'll catch him soon."

I hung up the phone. She wasn't sure of anything. She couldn't be. She couldn't protect me or keep

Eddie away from me. He hated me, that much was true, and he'd never forgiven me for Marisol.

I suddenly recalled Mariana's words to me.

You should run.

Chapter Three—Mariana McIntyre

I learned at an early age that my memory was quite superior to those of others. I could recall with near-perfect clarity the first song my governess ever sang to me. I remembered opening my first book; my chubby child's fingers struggled with the pages. I recalled taking my first pony ride, and I remembered the many times my father's soft whiskers brushed my cheek as he kissed me goodnight. Those memories I could easily summon, but the memory of my mother would forever elude me, and that filled me with a deep, gnawing sadness. Lillian Jane McIntyre, that was her name, lived to the age of eighteen and then died only six months after my birth. I felt a strange sense of guilt about her passing, although no one ever suggested that my arrival had anything to do with her death.

No. I could not remember her. But my brother Jameson claimed that he did. Although he was only two years older than I, the difference might as well have been a decade or a century. Jameson would never willingly speak about her, except to say she liked to wear black and rarely smiled. How could I believe such things? Most everything my older brother said was a horrible lie. And it saddened me to no end to see that Jacob would follow in his footsteps so well. More like his shadow. His long, cold shadow. For most of Jacob's life, I did my best to run interference between him and Jameson, to limit Jameson's influence over Jacob, but I had failed in my efforts. Even though Jameson mocked him and treated him more like a servant than a brother, Jacob adored him.

Jacob, that dear sweet boy, was only our half-brother—as Jameson so often reminded me. And although the youngest McIntyre clearly preferred our brother to me, I felt sympathy for him. His mother died too and not long after his birth. I did not miss my father's wife as much as I probably should. Ona McIntyre had not been a loving woman, and I wondered once more why my father had ever married her; once upon a time, he had been a very affectionate man. Ona lived at Pennbrook for only four years before the cough took her. Father had not remarried after that, and I was glad for it. According to Claudette Paul, my slightly older but not necessarily wiser friend, that made me the Lady of Pennbrook now.

I earnestly attempted to correct her, "Americans don't have lords and ladies, Claudette." She paid me no mind, and as I said, I secretly did not object to being the lady of the house. Even if I had lost my father's affection somewhere along the way.

But I didn't really have to guess when that happened, for I knew the moment precisely. I recalled it repeatedly with my perfect memory, seeing again the change in his expression, the shift in his face. Even his smile changed, at least when directed at me.

What a beauty your daughter has become, Mr. McIntyre! I imagine every respectable man in the county will want to see her for themselves.

Why would you imagine that, Mr. Chapman?

Mr. Chapman had been my father's lifelong friend and business partner but never received an invitation to return to Pennbrook after his generous compliment toward me. That had been well over a year ago. That's when the change happened. My father did not kiss my cheek anymore or applaud politely at my piano recitals or do any of the things he used to do. He looked at me quite differently. Not in an evil, diseased way, but in the way a man appraises a horse.

Yes, that was it. A new awareness arose in my father that day, and with it, the sun set on my childhood.

But maybe all things were made right again? This gift came, and so lovely a gift! I wished my mother could see this dress—or Claudette! She would come today and stay the week with me as we prepared for my birthday celebration. Mrs. Tutwiler, our most respectable neighbor, was also to help me with the preparations although I liked her company much less than Claudette's. I hugged the dress as I held it up to my reflection in the long mirror. It was a sumptuous rose-colored garment with far too many ruffles and ribbons woven into the sleeves. Oh, but I couldn't wait until Claudette arrived!

I suddenly took the notion to go show my mother my gift. A silly thing to do, I supposed, but my delight overpowered my thinking. My mother's painting hung in the downstairs study; it was a small painting without much detail. Lillian Jane had dark hair, as dark as mine, and she wore a pretty blue dress and a bright sunny smile. I did not believe my brother. He was one to lie just to please himself. Or to hurt me. One day his lying tongue would cost him if he wasn't careful. I told him as much yesterday; I warned him to keep quiet about things he knew nothing about. He went on and on about Father, one thing and then another. He'd been spying on our father, reading his mail whenever he left Pennbrook, which was quite frequently as of late. Jameson claimed to know some horrible secret that I did not. He taunted me at breakfast this morning, but I refused to encourage him. After a few bites I excused myself and took to the upstairs nursery hoping that Jacob would come, but he never showed. When my father returned, I would once again insist that he hire a governess for Jacob. Someone who could tame him, someone who would love him since he'd rejected me to please Jameson.

Clutching my gown, I raced down the stairs but halted outside the study. Someone was in Father's study, and I briefly hoped that my father had returned. It was not my father but Jameson sitting at his desk with the lamp lit, the room dark because of a gathering storm. He was once again elbow-deep in papers. Papers that did not belong to him.

"Ah, there she is. The Lady of Pennbrook. Good afternoon, sister."

I shuddered to hear him call me that. The only person who called me that had been Claudette. Did that mean my friend confided in Jameson too? I felt sick suddenly. "You've been talking to Claudette," I said.

It wasn't an accusation or a question. I just wanted him to know that I knew.

He didn't answer me but kept shuffling papers until he found what he was looking for. I stomped closer to him, angry now.

"What are you doing in Father's room, Jameson? I have told you before..."

He didn't appear to care about my warning. "You really should read this, dear sister. Here is your name, right here. Don't you care at all? Or are you happy to waste all your time sashaying about the house in ridiculous garments? If you are looking for ghosts, Mariana, they would not be in here."

I refused to take the bait Jameson dangled in front of me. How eager he was to always talk shamefully about our mother. He knew I would hate him for it, but he did it anyway. "I am sure if my name is on that paper, Jameson, there is a good reason for it. Now get out of the study, brother, before one of the servants finds you here and tells Father what you have been doing!" I cradled my gown tighter and suddenly felt foolish for coming in here at all.

What had I been thinking?

"And who would dare do that?" He glanced up at me, a curious expression on his plain face. Yes, he was plain, but he would certainly appear more handsome if he smiled occasionally. A real smile, not a devilish one. Not a sinister one. "What is that, sister?"

I held the garment to my flat bosom. "It is a gift for me. It came today; it is a dress, of course. A birthday gift from Father. He will want to see it when he arrives."

Suddenly he jumped up from behind the desk and came to examine the dress, like a moth to a candle. I saw that familiar gleam in his eye, the one that said, *I must take a snippet of that fabric. I must cut it,* but I snatched the gown away and tried to retreat from the study. "Where are you going, Mariana? Just let me look at the thing."

"Do not touch it!" I said. My voice sounded squeaky and frightened, just like a mouse cornered by a fat, hungry cat. My arguments would be useless. Once Jameson set his mind to a thing, he would have nothing else. I could never escape him or his strange demands. He was taller and faster, and my gown was too full and fluffy to hide away from him.

"Stop that struggling, sister. I will not hurt you. I never have, have I? Not really. Let me touch it. I just want to touch it." His voice was quiet now, but his grip was tight. I had no choice but to allow him to see my prize. Again I asked myself why I had come here.

"Please, do not destroy it, Jameson. Father will know. He bought this for me, brother. It is for my birthday. We will have a party in just a few days. Remember?"

"Oh, I won't destroy it, but you have to let me see it and allow me to take a small piece. Look at all these ribbons. You would not miss one, Mariana dear. All these touches. I do not have a ribbon this color, though your friend gives me ribbons all the time; she even allows me to cut her hair when I have need of it. I don't much care for your friend, Mariana. Her speech is not eloquent, and she smells of peppermint year-round. Oh, yes. I like this one. Just a little piece, please. I need a small sampling, I really do need it." His eyes were transfixed on the dress. He reminded me of a snake who had been charmed by the pipe of a snake charmer. I had seen such a scene myself in the pages of a book. Yes, he did look like a snake.

"You have need of nothing. Leave my gown alone. It is mine, Jameson." I slapped him as hard as I could. I had never struck him before, and he fell back on the desk clutching his face in surprise. I could see the handprint rising on his skin. I did not wait for his reply. He would surely make me pay for such an assault. Yes, he would make me pay in horrible ways.

With my dress in my hands, I ran up the stairs.

Chapter Four—Jerica

The sun beat down on me, and I wiped the sweat out of my eyes. I didn't like being up on this ladder, but if it prevented me heartache later, I'd just have to suck it up and do it. I'd made the drive to Mobile to pick up this alarm system; it wouldn't do me any good to leave it in the box. I half expected to see Jesse here and working on the interior of Summerleigh when I returned, but so far, he was a no-show.

Oh well. Probably for the best. I need a break to think about all this.

Why was I really objecting to Jesse's proposal? I mean, did I really want the whole bended-knee experience again? Look how well that worked out for me the last time. Eddie had written Will You Marry Me in the sand during our last night at the beach. To this day, I couldn't figure out how he did it because he'd never left my side the entire trip. He must have had someone scribble those words in the sand for him. I'd been so surprised when he fell on his knee and produced a ring. I never expected any of it, and I never thought twice about saying yes. I believed that I loved him and that everything was going to be okay.

Cut it out, Jer. Stop dreaming about the past.

With the power drill, I mounted the camera's brackets. I was so focused on my task and lost in my own thoughts, not to mention trying hard not to fall off the ladder, I didn't even hear Jesse pull in.

"Hey, what are you doing?" he called up to me out the window of his truck.

"Jesus!" I whispered, pretending that my knees didn't buckle in surprise. I kept my eyes on the bracket and then eased down the ladder, holding my breath the whole time. I pointed to the open box and removed the drill bit.

"So you aren't talking to me now?"

I put the camera and drill down. Wiping sweat from my face with the back of my hand, I sighed. "Of course I'm talking to you. You know I'm not good on ladders, and I'm trying to get this done before dark. Or is that a storm rolling in? Hot enough for it."

"This is a security system. Has something happened, Jerica? Did someone break into the cottage—or Summerleigh?"

"No. Nothing like that. It's just a precaution, just in case."

He laughed dryly and put the box back down. "In case what? After all the ghosts and the incident with Ben, what could you possibly be afraid of?" Then his smile disappeared. "Is this to keep me away? All you have to do is tell me, Jerica. I'm a big boy; I can handle the truth."

"I...uh. That's not what I'm doing, Jesse."

He reached for my arm as if to comfort me but thought better of it. "I know you, Jerica Jernigan. This isn't like you at all. Please, talk to me. Are you upset about my asking you to marry me? I have to admit, I wasn't expecting this response."

It didn't escape my notice that he used my maiden name and not my married one. *You can't erase my past by ignoring it, Jesse. And Eddie is my past.* "You didn't ask me, Jesse. You suggested it. Not the same thing." He leaned against the side of the house with his arms crossed over his chest now. Jesse's expression wasn't easy to read, but I recognized hurt when I saw it. He was hurt, and I was to blame. "This isn't about you. I would never install a security system to keep you away. It's Eddie. He's out of jail, and Detective Easton says he's coming here to Mississippi. I can only imagine why."

"What?" His arms bowed, and he was standing straight as a board. "Your ex is coming here? To Mississippi? Have I missed something?"

I shrugged in frustration. "That's what I said. I can't believe they are letting him out. On a technicality, no less. Once he leaves the state, they'll never find him. He's not going to be happy until..." I thought better of finishing that sentence. No need for dramatics. The situation was dramatic enough without the added histrionics.

"Have you heard from him? Has he threatened you?"

I put the drill back in the box and closed it up. "I haven't heard from Eddie and don't expect to. I have a new phone number. I won't hear from him, not until he shows up. And I expect he will do that. In his mind, we have unfinished business. He blames me for Marisol. He can't understand that it was an accident."

Jesse hugged me now, and I let him. It felt good to be close to him. Oh, God. I loved him. I did love him. "He's wrong, you know. You aren't to blame."

"Oh, I know. I was there. I remember every second of it. Every moment. It was not my fault, and Marisol knows that. She has moved on with Jeopardy. She's happy." I stepped out of his arms, refusing to cry. "Eddie has been high since she died. He just couldn't handle it."

"Let me help you with this. Then we can take a look at Summerleigh's security. Just in case. I'm not going to let him hurt you, Jerica."

"It's mostly done now. I've just got to set the software up on my tablet."

He began to walk to his truck like he wanted to roll up his window and stay a while. I would have liked nothing more, but the thought of Eddie showing up with Jesse here made me sick to my stomach. The idea of those two worlds colliding stressed me out. So like Eddie to want to contaminate everything good in my life. It was a wonder I'd kept my job at the Sunrise Retirement Home for so long.

"Jesse, go home. I've got this all buttoned up here. If you don't mind, we can finish up the crown molding tomorrow. I just need to think. I have to process all this."

"Are you sure you want to be alone?"

"I've been alone before, you know. I'm not afraid to be alone."

Jesse said in a soft voice, "Yes, but you don't *have* to be. Not this time."

I walked over to him, my wimpy ponytail sagging in the heat. I kissed him softly and whispered, "I don't need you to rescue me, Jesse. I have to do this. Me."

He kissed me back, but I knew he hoped to change my mind. He couldn't. If Eddie wanted me, I'd have to face him. I would defend myself. No more hiding and running. No more feeling like my life was spent at his mercy.

"I have to do this. This is my mess, Jesse. Not yours. I'll call you later. I promise."

"It's not like you to isolate yourself. Why are you shutting me out? What about supper? You want me to bring you something later?"

"No. I've got food. I'm not lying to you. I truly am fine. Go work on your boat and take a break from this house. And me."

"I don't need a break. Do you?"

"All I need is some time. Time to think about everything. That's all."

He paused, wavered in his boots for a minute and then climbed into the truck. With one last sad look, he shifted into reverse and drove away. His taillights glowed brightly in the growing darkness, and the smell of promised rain filled my nose. I glanced up at the sky in time to see lightning pulse through the clouds above me.

See there, Jesse Clarke. You don't know me at all.

Chapter Five—Jerica

At six o'clock on the dot, Jesse called me. I picked up the house phone happy to hear his voice. "Hey, Jesse."

"Hey. Just checking in. Did the security system work okay? You did set it for night vision, right?"

I tapped on the tablet screen and updated the settings without admitting I hadn't fine-tuned any of it. "It's working perfectly. I can see both porches." I tapped on the screen to see the other two cameras. "And the corners and even the wide-angle view. There's a good view of the back of Summerleigh too," I said as I flipped through all the angles.

"If anything goes off, any sound at all, any alarm, you call me. I mean it. I'm not happy about you being alone there. Maybe Ree-Ree should come stay with you tonight."

I smiled into the phone. "I will be just fine, Jesse Clarke. If I see anyone that remotely looks like Eddie Poole, I will call the sheriff's office first thing and then you. How does that sound?"

"Have you met our sheriff?"

I laughed at Jesse's insinuation. He had a strong distrust of any politician, big or small. And here in George County, the sheriff's office was a big point of contention for people who felt the same way. The conversation went silent between us. What should I say? Sorry? But I wasn't sorry.

"Ree-Ree needs me at the diner tonight. Something about Frank's big toe...dropped a can on it. I think he does stuff like that because he wants to get out of work. Why she keeps him around, I'll never know."

"Ouch," I said with a smile. "I've been promising to come to the diner to see her. I'll have to do that soon."

"Tonight's special is hamburger steak and gravy with a side order of mashed potatoes. My specialty," he said. I could hear the smile in his voice.

"I know what you're doing, tempting me with gravy and mashed potatoes, but I better stay here," I replied with a chuckle. And then I heard a weird beeping sound. It was the alarm system! I picked up the tablet and tapped on the screen as Jesse said his goodbyes. He asked me a question, but I wasn't paying attention.

"Okay, bye."

"Jerica? Are you listening to me at all?"

"Yeah. You said it was your specialty. I've got to go, Jesse. I've got something on the stove. Talk to you later." I hung up the phone and stared at the screen.

Nothing. I can't see anything. Wait a second. Doesn't this thing have a rewind button?

I had the cameras set to record anything that triggered the motion detector. I blindly tapped buttons, still unsure what button granted access to what feature. "Oh my God," I said as I stared at the tablet. There was a young man standing in my yard looking at my house. Looking at the camera! Then as quick as a flash of lightning, he was on my front porch. He was there one second and gone the next, but he was there for sure. I rewound the footage and watched it again.

I know that face! He looks so familiar!

And then my hair stood up. *Nobody disappears like that. Unless they aren't really there. Or aren't really alive. Oh my God! He's on my porch! Why had I hung up with Jesse?*

As I stared at the tablet in real time, my heart raced and my forehead broke out in a sweat again. I wasn't sure what to do. I'd had a ghost or two on my doorstep before. John Jeffrey Belle had even carried on a conversation with me. But I didn't get the feeling this man wanted to exchange pleasantries. He looked too angry for that.

I waited—for what, I did not know. I half expected the door handle to jiggle or doors to slam, but none of that happened. Instead, the phone rang. "Jesse Clarke, you're going to give me a heart attack," I whispered into the phone.

"I'm on the way. Don't open the door. Eddie is there, isn't he?"

I eased to the window and peeked out the curtain. There was no one there. No Eddie. No strange man with an angry face. "No. It was a false alarm. There is no one there. I think I may have set the sensitivity too high." *God, I'm horrible at lying.* "I'm adjusting the settings now."

"You aren't telling me something. What's really going on, Jerica?"

"Jesse, you're going to have to trust me. I'm fine. The alarm went off, but I've checked and there's no one there. I've got the doors locked, and I'm about to take a shower and cook some supper. Really. I'm perfectly fine." *I don't need you to rescue me, Jesse. I've been fine by myself for all these years*, I thought but didn't say.

"Alright. Well, call the diner if you need me." And he hung up, clearly unhappy with me.

I hung up the phone and retrieved my flashlight. I did need help, but not from Jesse.

I was going to have to find a way to connect with Harper. The only place I knew to find her was Summerleigh. I paused at the window and searched the yard for any evidence that the man with the angry face lingered. I didn't see him. *Well, now is as good a time as any.*

I left the safety of the cottage and walked across the yard. The air was dead still, and the sky had a strange, sepia quality to it. I felt as if I were walking in an old photograph of Summerleigh. There were white gardenias growing under the kitchen window, but there were no lights on inside.

Yes, I should go through the back door. If Harper was here, that was where I would find her.

I put the key in the lock and stepped inside.

Chapter Six—Mariana

"Mariana, of all the rooms here at Pennbrook, I think this one is my favorite, dearest. I am really surprised that you have not claimed it for yourself, as you should. Look at this view, and the new furniture is stunning. This is the new suite, correct? All the way from Bermuda? Ah, what a lovely see-dar scent." I tried not to notice Claudette's slight lisp, which tended to resurface whenever she became excited about anything. Even after all these years of regular speech lessons with marbles in her mouth, and after gargling with lemon juice and rubbing her neck with honey lotion, the lisp never truly disappeared. It was a fact that brought her much despair at times. No, it would not be kind to mention it now.

"Yes, it is lovely. Father had it delivered this week, along with a few other things. It has a peppery scent, very different from anything I have ever smelled," I said as we both rubbed our fingers across the red-tinted finish. I knew it was Bermuda cedar only because of Father's excitement about this particular line of wood furnishings. He owned the most successful lumber mill in south Mississippi but had quite recently entered the furnishings business along with his now-disfavored partner, Mr. Chapman.

"You know, as the lady of the house, you could move into this room. No one would say a word about it, not your servants or your brothers. Not even your father. If I were the Lady of Pennbrook, that is what I would do."

I shook my head in embarrassment at her reference to the title of "lady" yet again. Claudette appeared very fixated on such a silly thing, but I didn't argue with her.

"It has everything, Mariana. Shade in the afternoon, sunlight in the morning. You could sew in here, read and even paint. It is very well appointed, a picture of paradise. Much better than before, dearest." Her lisp resurfaced as her "dearest" became "dear-wist," but I smiled and nodded without flinching. I could not bear it if I caused her to break down in tears again on this particular subject.

I wondered at her assessment of the room, as I had not known her to spend much time in here previously, but I appreciated the suggestion. I most certainly agreed with Claudette's opinions, but I would never abandon my own rooms in the attic. It was home to me, and I had the entire floor to myself with plenty of space, even if it did have a tendency to get warm in the summer months. She sighed happily as she touched the blue floral wallpaper and closed her eyes to daydream about some romantic idea she had conjured in her own head. Claudette was a romantic, through and through. I sometimes felt like a character in one of her stories. She did like telling them, and I liked hearing them. Especially the one about the snake charmer and the sultan's daughter. I used to get lost in the stories she'd read to me when we were younger.

But we weren't alone in the room. Claudette's silent attendant, an older woman named Eliza, busied herself with emptying Claudette's trunk and boxes. It was as if Claudette planned to move in for a month, not spend the week with me. But then again, a lady could never have too many gowns, she would say. I watched in silence as the woman carefully removed one gorgeous dress after another, and I smothered the urge to race down the hall, retrieve my own new gown and show it to her. What a fight I had had with Jameson to keep it intact. But I had refused to open the door to him, and eventually Father called him away. No, showing off my new gown would not be polite, and I had other things on my mind. Besides, Claudette's wardrobe was far more impressive than mine and certainly more mature. I blushed at the sight of the plunging necklines and the sleeveless ball gown. I had no bosom to speak of at all. Father must have observed that, for my gown was embellished with a silk rose right where my nonexistent cleavage would have been. The stylish accent hid the noticeable lack of breasts. I could not stop staring at Claudette's wine-colored gown with the plunging neckline. She had the womanly figure that I did not.

Surely she intends to wear a wrap with that!

"Eliza, when you finish airing out the gowns, be sure to hang them up promptly so they do not wrinkle." The older woman nodded without looking in our direction, and Claudette settled in the chair next to the small round table in the corner of the room. "What time is your father joining us for dinner, Mariawana?" Her hand flew to her mouth as she tried to hide her embarrassment. I did as I always did and pretended nothing happened.

"I'm not sure. He's been very busy with his new business lately. I rarely see him anymore, dearest," I said with a polite smile.

She squeezed my hand and sighed and appeared quite pleased with her arrangements. "I do love this room." She released my hand and said, "Have you been to your father's new mill, Mariana? It is a triumph for him, you know. He truly is the captain of his industry." I wondered how she would know anything about it. Her father and mine were not friends, only neighbors, and I got the distinct impression that Mr. Anthony Paul was not one to mince words either. He was a judge on the Mississippi circuit and was gone much of the year on legal business.

"No, of course not. He has never invited me to visit the mill, nor do I expect he will do so." As usual, Claudette was two steps ahead of me when it came to gossip, even gossip about my own family. She knew something and was dying to tell me about it.

Just like Jameson.

"Claudette, I do not know anything about Father's business, but I would like to talk to you about something." I glanced in Eliza's direction as Claudette sighed and waved her away. The woman discreetly left us alone to the privacy of the blue floral guest room.

"What is it? What is on your mind, dear-wist? You know you can speak your heart to me." She patted my hand and smiled at me. She appeared so patient, even though she was less than two years older than me. Sometimes Claudette could be silly and petty and eager to share unkind secrets about her family, but she was probably my only true friend in the whole world. Once upon a time, Jameson and I had been friends, but we'd been much younger than we were now. And that was before he began to tell his lies.

"It is about Jameson, Claudette. I have questions, and I need you to be honest."

Her hazel eyes grew wide, and I could see she was curious. "Of course I would be honest with you, my true friend. You know I am your friend, dearest Mariana. I shall always be your friend and will always tell you the truth. What is on your mind? Come now, hold nothing back. You can talk to me as if I were your true sister."

"Is it true that you and my brother will marry? That you have romantic feelings for him?"

Her hand flew to her chest. She had such long, slender fingers. I could see that she was not expecting my question, and immediately I knew that I was not going to like her answer for she paled and her pale pink lips stretched into a pained smile. My friend had light olive skin, bright hazel eyes and light brown hair. I noticed that her straight hair was losing its curl; she wanted so desperately to have springy curls like my own, or at least so she said on many occasions. I had always thought that Claudette was a handsome young woman but not quite pretty. Certainly not beautiful but intelligent, humorous and even accomplished. She was in every way my equal even though my family was wealthier than hers by half. In the world that Claudette and I shared, those differences were very important. What young woman didn't want to be considered beautiful or polished in her manners?

"Surely you must know, Mariana, that I will eventually marry, as will you. We are young women of marriageable age now, and of course our families will want us to marry and have our own families. Is it so offensive to you to think of me as your true sister? Would you object if I did marry into your family? For then, we would truly be sisters."

"You know that I love you as I love my own family, but my brother is not well, dearest. He does things that are not normal." I noticed that Claudette's hand went to her ear, and I quickly discerned that a lock of her hair was missing.

So it was true, then!

Then Claudette was on her feet, her hands curled into fists. I never expected such a defensive posture from her. "I have lis...lis...tened to you dis-cwedit your brother long enough, and I can do it no longer." Not only was her lisp on full display, but she stuttered as well. I hoped for her sake that did not mean she would have a seizure. She rarely had them, but when she did, she would sleep for days afterward and wake up with bloodshot eyes and no memory of soiling herself. I prayed for her sake that it did not happen during my birthday party.

But she would not relent. "No. I mean this, Mariana. Whatever displeasure you have held with your brother needs to end. Why must you insist on seeing the worst in him when there is good there also? Why? Is it because of Jacob? He is the one who is disturbed. Do you not understand that?"

It was my turn to spring to my feet; my gown made a strange hissing noise as the layers of fabric settled around me like an angry cloud. "It is true, then. You are positioning yourself to marry my brother behind my back!"

"That is not true, Mariana!"

"All this time I thought you were my friend. But it turns out you were more interested in becoming Jameson's *bwide*." And in that moment, I did mean to mock her. It felt good to be hateful about her speech impediment. And if it hurt her, it was her own fault. She'd done this to herself.

Claudette took a deep breath and shoved her hands in her skirt pockets. "Stop that, Mariana. You promised you would never mock me. I'm not doing anything of the sort. And as far as I know, nothing has been arranged for me; there has only been talk, and not just about me but about you too. Your father has already begun your marriage arrangements, or have you not heard? I can only hope to marry someone as wonderful as a McIntyre. Now if you don't mind, I would like to be alone to *west* before dinner. Pw...please send my servant in," she struggled to finish her sentence coherently. Claudette turned her thin back to me and stood before the open window. I wanted to talk more about this, to argue with her and explain my position, but she was having none of it and did not turn around. I was so shocked and overwhelmed by what I'd learned that I could hardly argue with her.

To think, Jameson had told me the truth!

"Very well. I shall leave you to your rest," I whispered. I walked out the door and found Eliza leaning against it. I didn't bother telling her that she should go in, for she had been eavesdropping and already knew this.

As I stumbled down the hall with tears in my eyes, I shook my head at the news. Would my father make arrangements for my hand to someone I did not know? And if it was someone I knew, who was it?

Jameson knew. I was sure of that now. I had to know! Who would I marry, and why was I the last to know? And why would Claudette want to marry my brother? She knew about his...perversions, his incessant need to cut at the things he admired.

I walked down the hallway lost in my thoughts when I heard Jacob's voice. He wasn't talking or giggling as he had a tendency to do whenever something amused him; he was reciting poetry. Sir Walter Scott, if I wasn't mistaken. That was something I had never been able to achieve with him. Perhaps Father had sent for a governess after all?

I was beginning to understand that many things happened at Pennbrook that I was unaware of. I would surely have heard about a new governess' arrival, wouldn't I? I walked toward the nursery door and was shocked to see Jacob and Jameson sitting together on the long blue settee. Jacob had an open book in his lap and was flipping the page as I paused to listen. He read a little more, not perfectly but much better than before. Obviously, he'd been practicing. And that's when Jameson saw me. He was holding a tiny pair of scissors and cutting into a stack of folded paper. Making paper dolls was an old hobby of his. I was surprised to see him working at it again.

"Continue," he said to my brother as he rose and walked toward the door. I thought about what to say to him, what to do. Should I apologize to him? Offer him some sort of peace offering? I hardly knew how to proceed. I felt lost, in a whirlwind, in a place where I had no control over anything. Jameson walked toward me, a wooden expression on his face. It was like I was invisible, like I wasn't there at all. Was I a ghost? There was no welcoming smile on his face, not a trace of triumph.

And then he closed the door.

Chapter Seven—Jerica

My exploration of Summerleigh availed me nothing. Whatever ghost or spirit showed up in my surveillance video wasn't in the house now, and there was no sign that Harper was there either.

Where are you, Harper?

I was trained in grief management. Grief counseling had been a part of my job when I worked at the Sunrise Retirement Home. Although I didn't want to admit it, I was beginning to suspect that a lot of my emotional uncertainty lately stemmed from the fact that I had not given myself time to mourn Harper. She'd been such an integral part of my life, especially during the loss of Marisol and afterward. Harper had been such a friend to me, almost a mother, that it seemed impossible to think I would never see her again.

I mean, I knew she had passed away. I understood the concepts of life and death and mourning and grief. From the day she died until recently, Harper remained a part of my life in a strange, metaphysical way. But she was gone now. Yes. That was a fact that could not be denied. She was gone, and I had to move on with my own life.

Maybe Ben Hartley had been right. Maybe it was Summerleigh itself that brought the melancholy out in me and in all who called the place home. I wasn't sure, and I didn't have all day to think about it. Trucks were pulling up in the yard. Jesse. Emanuel and Renee were converging on Summerleigh as I pondered life in my kitchen. With a frown, I finished the dregs of this morning's coffee. That's when I heard a tap on the front door.

"Coming," I called. Renee was there waiting for me with a big smile on her face and a gift in her arms. It was wrapped in tissue with a big pink bow on it.

"Brought you something, sweetie. I couldn't wait for you to come to the house; I had to give it to you now."

I smiled at her thoughtfulness. "I'm just headed that way now. Can we go over there, or should we open it here?"

"If you are ready to go, let's head to Summerleigh. That's where this belongs, anyway." Renee's long dark hair was piled on top of her head in a casual yet perfect messy bun. As usual, she sported flawless makeup and like me wore shorts and a t-shirt even though it was November. When was fall going to arrive?

"How did you get time off from the diner? I wasn't sure you were going to be able to join me with Frank's swollen toe."

She rolled her eyes. "Just lucky, I guess. And I told Frank that if he had one more injury, I was gonna fire him. He's always dropping something or cutting something or setting something on fire. I swear, the man is a danger to himself and my business."

I poked her in the side playfully. "But you are crazy about him, aren't you?"

"What can I say? I have a weakness for klutzes."

We went into the kitchen and said a quick hello to Jesse, who was busy going over the furniture placement chart with Emanuel. There were others in the house too, craftsmen polishing up various projects, but the work was largely complete. For the first time, I could see the rainbow at the edge of the storm, and my dream of restoring Summerleigh was close to coming to fruition.

Most of the furniture would arrive today, and the interior decorating was starting. This was my least favorite part, but Renee had proved repeatedly that she had an eye for those kinds of details. And Jesse knew all the historical touches that needed to be added. Not to mention I'd seen this place as it used to be many times in the dreams that Harper shared with me.

Oh, Harper. I wish you could see this place now. If you can see me, find a way to let me know.

I heard nothing but Renee chattering beside me. I followed her to the nearest guest room, which would've been Harper's old bedroom. There was a wrought iron bed with a new mattress, a curtainless window and a shabby-chic dresser against the wall.

"Go ahead. Open it." Renee was so excited, I could hardly say no.

I unwrapped the tissue and tugged on the ribbon to release the surprise. "Renee, this is the most gorgeous thing I've ever seen. I love it. What a beautiful quilt!"

"I'm so glad you like it. My neighbor Betsy works on quilts on the side, and I thought this would be perfect for Harper's room. Don't you love those cherries? That's a retro print. Feel the weight? Makes me want to snuggle up with it right now. If it wasn't so warm."

I spread the fabric out to get a good view of the complicated patchwork. "I love it, but I'm not sure I can accept this. This had to set you back a bit. I mean, look at this workmanship. Really, Renee, it's too much."

"I don't think you understand the meaning of the word 'gift,' Jerica. This is my late birthday and early Christmas gift to you. Now let's put it on the bed. I even brought sheets to go with it. I'm dying to see what it looks like in here." Renee's big smile made it impossible for me to refuse her thoughtful gift. I would never have dreamed of putting something like this on the bed, but Renee was right, those vintage cherries were perfect for Harper's room. She used to have a dresser with cherry embellishments, and I knew for a fact that she always loved that romper of Jeopardy's. We spread the quilt over the freshly sheeted bed and sat back in amazement. It looked perfect.

I wiped a tear from my eye and said, "Harper would have loved this. I love it, Renee. Thank you." It wasn't like me to dole out hugs, but I couldn't help but hug her. We were both teary-eyed as Jesse walked in the room, his eyes gleaming with excitement and not about the quilt. He had a dusty box in his hand.

"Look what I found in the attic. Can you believe this? I guess you know who this must have belonged to. After all this time, I found it."

Staring at the dusty wooden box, I knew exactly what he was talking about. This belonged to Jameson McIntyre! This was the very treasure box that Jacob and Jameson had been protecting. "Let's go into the kitchen and open it, Jesse. It's too dusty to open it in here. Did you see the gorgeous quilt Renee brought?"

Jesse complimented Renee, and together the three of us headed to the kitchen to look inside the treasure box. With shaking hands, he put it on the table and opened it. I don't know what I was expecting, maybe a box of little skeletons or bottles of poison or pieces of hair or maybe even bloody garments, but that wasn't what I saw. There were a few ribbons and, yes, a curl or two of hair, but besides that it was nothing like I expected. There were some pieces of paper, and I picked one up and began to read it. "You are cordially invited to attend..."

Jesse broke in and said, "This is for Mariana's birthday party. It's an old invitation! This must have been written around the time when she was murdered. Why would he keep this?"

I tried to read the faded writing, but it was difficult. "Look, guys. It says Pennbrook. Could that be the name of the old house before they rebuilt it? Is that the original Summerleigh? I've never heard of Pennbrook before. Have you, Jesse?"

"No, I haven't, but that doesn't mean anything. Remember, all of those old records were lost. Pennbrook doesn't ring a bell, but now I have something to research. With this name and maybe some of this other information, I can turn up something."

Renee swallowed and said, "I hope finding this box doesn't stir things up around here. I'd be really worried for you if it did. Are you sure everything is okay, Jerica? You seem a little distracted today."

"Well, I did see someone on my porch last night, a young man. But it wasn't a living person because he vanished into thin air. He was standing in the yard, and then quick as a flash, he appeared on the porch. And then he vanished. I thought it must be a glitch with the camera, but I've never heard of a glitch projecting an image that isn't actually there."

Jesse asked, "What did he look like?"

"He looked a bit like Jacob; I think it may have been Jameson, but I can't be sure. A shadow obscured his face, like he was deliberately trying to hide his identity from me. Sounds crazy, huh?"

Renee let out a sigh. "Please, from what we know of this place, that doesn't sound crazy at all. It sure doesn't surprise me. What about you, cousin?"

Jesse was staring at me accusingly but said nothing. He closed the box and said, "I'd like to take this home and check it out later if you don't mind. But in the meantime, we've got furniture trucks arriving, and I think the telephone guy is here. Can you show him where to install everything while I help Emanuel move the furniture around?"

"I'll do the bossing," Renee said sweetly in an attempt to lighten the mood. The installation man was walking in, and I quickly greeted him. For the next hour, we were all so busy that I didn't have much time to think about the contents of the box or anything that had to do with Pennbrook or the McIntyre family. The tech knew his business and quickly ran the necessary lines we would need for the house.

"You guys have it looking great in here. Must be exciting to see an old place brought back from the dead. I always wanted to see it fixed up."

I smiled at his choice of words. "Yes, we're all very happy about it." I heard the furniture trucks drive away and peeked out the window to see the dusty air stirring up behind the exiting vehicles. Renee poked her head in and said, "I've got to get to the diner, but I think everything is where it should be. See you later."

That was disappointing. I had hoped to spend more time with my optimistic friend, but I couldn't keep her here forever. "Sounds great. Thanks for your help, Renee. And thanks again for the gift!" I called to her as the kitchen door closed. To my surprise, Jesse's truck cranked up too. Either he was still upset with me or he had that box on the brain and wanted to go home to start plundering it in earnest.

Maybe I would surprise him with a visit? No. Probably not. I was the one who wanted some space.

Either way, it quickly became apparent that the phone installation man and I were the only ones left at Summerleigh. I followed him into the Great Room, and we watched the modem finally light up. He tested the connection on his tablet, and I signed the appropriate paperwork. Yes, it was all quiet in here now.

"Yeah, this is a real nice place you have here, Mrs. Poole."

I blinked at hearing that name. I might need to have that changed soon. I never wanted to think of being a Poole ever again. "Please call me Jerica."

"My older sister is getting married next summer, and she's been looking for a place for the reception. This looks like it would be large enough to have a nice wedding reception. I see you guys are going to be open soon. Would it be possible to get a business card or brochure or something?" The words had barely left his lips when we heard footsteps above us.

It was the sound of high heels clicking across the wooden floor upstairs. I could have played it off as normal, pretended that there was someone up there walking around in old-fashioned high heels, if not for the extreme coldness invading the room and the absolute feeling of wrongness that overwhelmed me. And by the look of the tech, he was feeling it too. His expression was all the assurance I needed that there was something supernatural happening right this very moment.

"I can get you a card. I have some in my purse. Be right back." Anxious to keep things normal and to pretend that there was nothing happening, I scurried off into the kitchen, opened a cabinet door and dug out a card from my purse. It took me more than a few seconds to find one, and when I returned to the Great Room the installation man was gone. And I hadn't even heard the door open or close. The paperwork was on a nearby table, but beyond that there was neither hide nor hair of him. And then I heard the truck pulling away.

I don't know why, but that really ticked me off. We were doing so much around here, so much work, we'd put in so much effort to bring life back to Summerleigh. We'd worked hard to clear the proverbial air and help those spirits that wanted to be helped. And now it looked like my work wasn't done yet.

"Great. Just great," I said to the empty house. But it wasn't empty. Who was I kidding?

Obviously, I was talking to the ghost of Mariana McIntyre.

Chapter Eight—Jerica

With my princess telephone in my hand, I dialed Hannah's number but then quickly hung up. Was I ready to get involved with the psychic again? Would she even take my call? This wasn't the time to do that. I was a big girl, as I kept telling Jesse. It was time to take things into my own hands. I washed the supper dishes and put them back in the cabinet knowing all the while exactly what I was going to do. I took the key off the latch and headed out the door toward Summerleigh. There were no phantom lights glowing in the windows, no shadowy figures and no beckoning ghosts. Just the growing sense that I wasn't alone.

And that I was expected.

But by whom? That was the question.

I half expected to see my boyfriend's beat-up old truck tooling down the driveway, but it didn't happen. Well, at least he was respecting my wishes. What more could a girl want?

I slid the key in the back door, opened it and stepped inside to enjoy the view. The renovated kitchen was inspiring. We put so much work into restoring those old details that it really felt as if one of the Belles might come in at any moment and invite me to help make a pan of biscuits. A stack of white and blue china plates waited neatly in the glass front cabinets, and there were jelly jars in a basket on the counter along with a collection of colorful red and white napkins. It was a lovely space with precious details.

We would open the Summerleigh Bed-and-Breakfast in a few weeks, just in time for the holiday season. It was exciting, tiring and nerve-racking all at once. Word had gotten out around town about the new venture, and we already had a few reservations thanks to Renee, who was really skilled at drumming up business. I was glad about the prospect of money coming in. Although Jesse and I were technically partners, I was footing the lion's share of the bills. But that's not to say he wasn't doing his share of the work. Nobody could ever say that Jesse Ray Clarke wasn't a hard worker.

I moved a few of the items around the countertops before walking into the parlor. We had not been successful in acquiring one of those old radios, but we found a nice reproduction and the space was roomy, perfect for entertaining multiple guests. Jesse and I had toyed with the idea of hosting some historical chats in this room. In my mind, I could see Ann Marie Belle perched on the couch, her knees tucked up under her, giving me a disapproving look while she absently thumbed through a magazine and looked bored.

For some reason, I felt like something was out of place in this room, not quite right. I moved a few things around but couldn't shake the feeling. *I'll think about it some more.* Then I stepped into the empty Great Room. The fireplace was beautifully restored and filled with vanilla-scented candles. The bookcases were painted white and stuffed with interesting pieces that we'd discovered in the attic. It was a nice room but not as cozy as the parlor. I walked through and headed to the hallway that led to the bedrooms. I smelled paint and carpet adhesive; strangely enough, it was a satisfying combination.

I went into Harper's room, amazed again at the beauty of Renee's quilt. Everything was in order in here, I thought as I flipped on the light and glanced around the room. In fact, besides hanging an odd picture or two, I checked the room off in my mind. Yes, this room was perfect. Besides the kitchen, Harper's room was the one that made me completely happy. I had to pinch myself—this wasn't a dream. This was my life, and it was a good one. I took a quick survey of the other rooms and then headed up the stairs. No one silently stalked me, but then again, the boy ghost was gone now. I paused in the hallway outside the nursery door and shivered, then took a deep breath and stepped into the room.

Nope. It was still uncomfortable in here, despite the fresh paint, the new door and the new light fixtures. So uncomfortable. I wasn't convinced that any amount of redecoration would help this place. It had been here that I'd offered the ghost boy Marisol's purple bear. Shaking my head and rubbing my arms against the chill, I left the room and closed the door behind me. The other bedrooms on this floor were neat and tidy with new hardwood flooring and period furniture but with modern touches like electric lamps and top-of-the-line mattresses. I especially liked the room that overlooked the backyard. It had a comfortable, peaceful feeling. I went into that room, shifted a small table, placed a book of poetry on the nightstand and left, happy with the arrangements. The other rooms were nice but not completely furnished yet. And then my eyes fell on the attic.

Jesse and I had decided to keep this room private. It had a new door with a lock, and although we had spent a great deal of time cataloging and storing many of the antiques up here, there was plenty of stuff left. No, we could never rent this room out.

This would always be Jeopardy's room. And also Mariana's, I suddenly thought. That knowledge inspired me.

"Mariana, are you here? It's me, Jerica. I'm not here to disturb you. I just want to talk to you." I sat on a nearby stack of plastic tubs and waited. Why hadn't I thought to bring a digital recorder up here? Hadn't I learned anything about paranormal investigation? I should be an old pro by now.

I watched the sun go down, and the room darkened quickly. I felt apprehensive but not fearful. I expected to see or hear Mariana; I talked a bit more and invited her to speak with me, but in the end, nothing happened. There was the groaning of the old attic floor, the occasional shifting of the air, but no ghost, no voice, nothing at all.

Leaving the attic behind, I retraced my steps to make sure I'd turned off all the lights. Everything was in order here on the top floor. I was tempted to head back home but on a whim decided to check out the bottom floor too. Turning off the light in the Great Room, I hurried down the hall that led to the bedrooms. The only light on was Harper's.

Hmm...I don't think I left that on. Maybe...

I pushed open the door and waited. Nobody was there, but something had changed.

The quilt had been turned down, just like Harper used to do right before bed. Like she used to do for all her sisters and her mother. I walked toward the bed, wide-eyed and holding my breath. With shaking fingers, I touched the cool fabric and glanced over my shoulder.

"Harper?" I asked as I sat on the edge of the bed. But I didn't really have to ask. I knew what this was.

This was an invitation.

I wasn't remotely tired, but I kicked off my shoes and slid under the quilt. After thirty minutes of waiting and watching, my eyes grew heavy and I fell asleep.

Chapter Nine—Mariana

The night before my party, Father came home, and he was in a fine mood. He was happy and kind and loving to me once again. I couldn't understand the change in his attitude. Father did not avoid me, or at least he did not avoid looking into my eyes. He even dressed for dinner and wore a new, dark blue suit, refrained from smoking at the table and drank only one glass of brandy when offered to him. To be fair, though, his cheeks were quite red during our dinner, as if he had previously imbibed. I noticed he carried a new gold watch that he repeatedly removed from his pocket to check the time. He laughed, and Claudette gave me an awkward shrug. I felt like I was missing some secret, but I could not discern it.

At least the letter sent by Mrs. Tutwiler explained why she had been absent. Her own son Donnie had pneumonia, and the prognosis was not hopeful. Donnie was a nice boy with blond hair and big blue eyes; he was as stupid as Old Edward, Father's stable hand, but it would be sad to lose him. I prayed silently for him as we waited for the first course of our dinner.

As the pumpkin soup was served, Jameson gave me a sideways smile at seeing my confusion. He and Father talked a good long time about the furniture business, and Claudette asked a few polite questions about Bermuda and the processing of the cedar from that wild place. Their chatter continued through the soup service, to the pork loin and potatoes and through the dessert, a vanilla pudding with caramel sauce. I realized that I was not as hungry as I had expected to be. I sat as quietly as a porcelain doll and listened to them talk to one another, almost as intimately as Claudette and I might from time to time.

Then my father remembered his manners and complimented me on my dark green gown. He asked if the new rose gown pleased me, and I shot a look at Jameson that said, *See there? I told you he wouldn't want the gown cut up.*

"It is a fine dress, Father. Fit for a queen."

"Or the Lady of Pennbrook, Mr. McIntyre," Claudette added.

"Please, call me Michael. Or Bull, whichever you prefer," he said, tipping his glass to her. I was shocked to see him then squeeze her hand briefly. His face flushed as he released her.

She touched her face with the hand he touched and leaned forward slightly. I heard her whisper, "I pwefer Michael."

Any sympathy I may have felt for her regarding her handicap had vanished. I suddenly hoped that she would lisp and stutter her way through the rest of dinner.

What is going on here?

I sat quietly as Father pretended to be a young man and flirt with my oldest and dearest friend. I felt sick, sick like a cat that had eaten a bad mouse. In fact, I wanted nothing more than to throw up and go to bed. Surely I had entered a nightmare.

Rising to my feet suddenly, I said, "Please excuse me, Father. I do not feel well. I think I need to rest until this passes."

"Should I call for the doctor?" my father asked, seeming genuinely concerned about me; it was the first time he had really noticed me at all tonight.

"No, Father." I pressed the white linen napkin to my lips to prevent myself from becoming ill. "Please enjoy your dinner. I am going to bed. Thank you for the gift."

"I will walk you up, dear sister."

"No thank you, Jameson. I can walk just fine."

"Let your brother help you, Mariana. Jacob, stay right where you are. You promised to read to Claudette, did you not?"

Jacob gave both Jameson and me a distrustful glance but did as he was told. Luckily for him, he had brought the book with him; he stood beside the table and began to recite. As I walked up the stairs with Jameson beside me, I heard Father and Claudette applauding politely.

"When did he learn to recite so well? Did you teach him?"

"No, the real teacher around here is Claudette, don't you agree? Is that really the question you want to ask me?"

Clutching my wobbly stomach, I whispered, "I must confess this whole night has been confusing to me, from the beginning to now." I opened the door to my bedroom, thankful that I had hidden my new dress so well that Jameson would never find it. Let him cut on one of my other gowns but not that one.

"Shall I tell you what you didn't want to hear before? Shall I tell you the truth, even though it is unpleasant, at least for you?"

"Tell me what you want to tell me, Jameson."

"Why should I? What are you going to give me?" His snake's smile returned to his face. He glanced around and could not find my dress, but I knew he wanted to see it. "Oh, never mind. Even though you treated me harshly before, I will tell you what I know, and then maybe you will give me what I want. Miss Claudette Paul has set her cap at our father, Mariana. Not me. She has no desire to marry me, nor do I have any desire for her. We talked about it once briefly when she was twelve, and we both decided it would never work. But she does like to please me sometimes and offers her hair or a ribbon as a kind of peace offering between us. And you should know, dearest Mariana, she wants nothing less than to be the Lady of Pennbrook. It's all she ever talks about, sister. She doesn't want me at all but our father; she wants to be a McIntyre. Now why that is, I don't know."

"Why would he want to marry again? He has the three of us. He does not need any other children."

"He is a man, by all accounts a young, virile man, and he needs a good wife to run his house and do the things a wife should do besides merely have children. I wonder at your intelligence at times, Mariana."

I banged my hand on the wall. "I don't believe a word you tell me, Jameson Michael. I don't believe you at all!" I said as I went to close my door. I did feel dizzy now, on top of being sick.

"Be a fool, then! You're nothing if not consistent!" Then he muttered, "Stupid girl," under his breath and stomped away still mumbling.

I slammed the door and climbed into bed. Once the room stopped spinning, I fell asleep.

Chapter Ten—Jerica

A feather rubbed across my nose. Or something. What was that? I opened my eyes and discovered it was a lock of my hair tickling my face. My eyes popped open as I recalled my surroundings.

I was sleeping in Harper's bed. But I hadn't seen my friend or any of her sisters; I dreamed of someone else last night. I dreamed of Mariana McIntyre—a young woman who had been dead for 150 years. With my eyes closed, I attempted to recall every second of the shared memory, for I had no doubt that my late friend was somehow involved in the paranormal experience. Or maybe it wasn't Harper at all. Maybe it was simply Summerleigh. Maybe it had been Summerleigh's power all this time. No. I didn't want to believe that. I hoped with all my heart to be reconnected with Harper at least one more time, just to say goodbye. But it hadn't happened. Not yet. I pushed back the quilt and sat up and stretched. As comfortable as this bed was, it was no substitute for my own. What had I been thinking?

I listened quietly and hoped to hear footsteps pattering around upstairs, maybe children's footsteps or high heels like those that had belonged to Mariana. But I heard nothing. It was as if the house had fallen asleep and slept still.

Harper, if you're trying to show me something, I don't get it. I know that Jameson murdered his sister. I don't want to witness it if I don't have to. Harper? Can you hear me?

I sighed at the lack of noise and climbed out of bed. I'd left my toothbrush and toothpaste and all of my personal items back at the caretaker's cottage, so I would have to go home if I wanted to tidy up for the day ahead of me. I made the bed quickly and fluffed the pillows. Yes, everything seemed normal.

Quiet.

Dead.

And then I saw the picture. It was a wedding picture, an old black-and-white photo in an even older picture frame. Despite the faded color and some minor damage to the photo, I could see every face plainly. This was the day that Addison married Frank! I had seen this moment in a dream. Harper had shown it to me! I remembered the moment that she looked up at the attic and saw the Lady in White staring down at her. Mariana's lips had been moving, but I couldn't make out the words at all.

This picture hadn't been here before; I was sure I would have known if it had been. I would have adored this picture; I was just in here with Renee yesterday, and we would've seen it. But it had not been here, so who put it here? That was the question. I took it off the wall and examined the back of it, then popped off the back of the frame and searched for clues, but there was nothing to see. No inscription, no faded words on the back of the picture. But I knew those faces. I loved those faces.

And then it occurred to me—Harper wanted me to see this picture. She had wanted me to spend the night here. This picture was here for my benefit, but what did it mean? As I stared harder at the scene, taking my time to identify as many of the details as I could, my phone rang and startled me.

I answered it without looking. I was too busy staring at the picture. "Hello?"

"Good morning, Jerica. This is Detective Easton. I'm calling to follow up on the status of your ex-husband, Eddie Poole."

I tore my eyes away from the picture and focused on the phone call. I really needed to listen to what she had to say. My life might depend on it. "I'm all ears, Detective. What's the latest?"

"Eddie is definitely on the move. And to make matters more complicated and ten times more dangerous, he has a gun. He robbed a convenience store and a package store just this morning, and by the way he's traveling, it is clear to me that he is on his way to you."

"Great. Just great. How many crimes does he have to commit before he gets caught?" I sat on the bed trying to catch my breath.

She agreed with me but didn't seem eager to hang up. That made it even worse because I only ever heard from Easton when something horrible was happening. Like this, for example. "Eddie is disturbed in a very real and dangerous way, Jerica. I think you need to move. Go somewhere safe."

"You aren't telling me anything I don't already know about my ex-husband. I was a fool for a long time but not anymore. I am not going anywhere. I did that once before, remember? I have a gun and a security system; I am going to stand my ground, Detective."

Her voice deepened and took on a more serious tone. "You are playing with fire, ma'am. He's made several threats online; some are quite disturbing. I think I should read a few of them to you so you understand..."

"I'm not on social media, Detective. That would mean nothing to me. So what if he's making threats? He's been threatening me for years. I'm sure this won't be the last time either." Who was I kidding? I didn't take this news nearly as lightly as I was pretending, but this detective was going to be of no help to me. None at all. Might as well get rid of her now. "I know that he wants to harm me, that he blames me for Marisol's death, but he's wrong, you know. He's wrong." I hadn't expected it, but I started crying. I cried because once upon a time, I had loved Eddie Poole; we made a beautiful and magical child together. *I am so sorry, Marisol.* Marisol's death ended all of that, not the love I had for her but my marriage. Her death ended our family, and it was a grief I felt deeply. And I knew that Eddie did too in his own way. In his own warped way.

"I have to make a few phone calls. Goodbye, Detective. Thank you for calling me, but I'm sure I will be okay."

"I am calling the local sheriff's department for you, Jerica. They have to know what they're up against. It would be wrong of me not to prepare them for the violence they may encounter if they try to apprehend this man. He is dangerous to more than just you. He is dangerous to the community at large. You should know something else too." She paused as if she wanted me to ask her what that something was. I wasn't sure I wanted to, so I waited for her to continue speaking.

"Eddie is addicted to heroin. I'm sorry to tell you that, but it's the truth. When he's desperate, he will shoot pills or whatever he can get his hands on. If we don't catch him, I don't think you'll live very long. He's got a death wish. Have you ever heard of something called suicide by cop?"

"I think so."

"Well, the doctor thinks that Eddie is a prime candidate for this type of thing. Please be careful."

I rubbed my nose with the back of my hand and promised to do just that before hanging up on her. She was still talking, but there was nothing left to say and nothing I wanted to hear.

I walked out of Summerleigh and locked the door behind me. Renee had not arrived yet. It was only around 6:30 in the morning, and she didn't usually show until about 7:30.

But I knew who would be awake. Jesse was always awake this early. I picked up the phone and dialed.

"Hey, I need your help with something. I want you to teach me how to shoot, and I might actually need to buy a gun."

"Does this mean that he's—nope. I don't really want to know, but I do believe that you should be prepared...especially if you're going to keep me away, which I don't understand at all."

"Will you just answer the question? Will you teach me how to shoot?"

"Of course I will. You want to get started now?"

"There's no time like the present," I said as I quoted my father.

"Okay, let me stop by the bank and get my gun out and grab some bullets at the hardware store. Be there in about an hour. Are you cooking breakfast?" I could hear the grin in his voice.

"I guess I could try."

"Nope. Why don't you let me bring something? I'll be there in about an hour with breakfast and anything else you might think of. Just text me. And Jerica?"

"Yeah?"

"Thank you for letting me help you."

"Yeah. I'm an idiot. Thanks for coming to my rescue." And then I added, "I love you, Jesse Clarke." I don't know why I said it, but I did, and I didn't regret it. I hung up before he could answer me.

Time to get ready to face the day. Whatever it might bring.

Chapter Eleven—Mariana

My bedroom brightened as the clouds skittered away on an invisible breeze. The half-moon above cast strange shadows in the corners of my room, and I felt I could no longer trust my eyes. I saw spirits everywhere, phantoms that looked like my mother. And other things. Darker, more frightening. But as quickly as I saw them, they vanished like smoke.

More than once, I suspected that someone was watching me, but surely that was only a feeling. Earlier, my doorknob rattled and a tapping on the wall beside my bed startled me; I assumed the noises came from my former friend. I refused to open the door or respond to her tapping or open my heart to her again if this was her. And it must be!

No. I would not make that mistake twice. My mind raced back to the moment at the dinner table. I could see Claudette rubbing her skin, obviously relishing my father's light touch on her wrist. Such an intimate and disgusting moment. How could my father play the fool with such a foolish girl? *Claudette, how could you betray me?*

My nose was runny from my earlier crying jag, and I wiped at it as I sat in the chair near the window. Occasionally, deer wandered across the grassy lawn and nibbled their way to the pond. Perhaps I would see one tonight. I did so enjoy watching them. Such peaceful animals. Goodness knows I needed something to distract me from my rumbling stomach. My sickness had vanished, and in its place I felt a raw hunger. I waited and toyed with the soft bristles of my brush as I watched the shadows move on the ground below. I saw nothing. Not a deer or a squirrel.

Nothing at all except Jacob.

My younger brother ran awkwardly across the lawn wearing nothing but his nightshirt. What was he doing? Jacob knew the pond was off-limits to him without one of us to watch him. My father had always been so adamant about that. Oh, why hadn't Father hired a governess? I could not be expected to watch over Jacob when he refused to listen to me.

I reached for my robe and threw it over my body as I raced toward the door and fumbled with the cold key. The heavy lock clunked, and the door opened to the chilly hallway. Hurrying as quickly and quietly as possible, I rushed down the stairs and out of the house. I saw no one and heard nothing except the chiming of the clock and the light scampering of a mouse. Even though our home was new, there were mice in the walls. Many mice. I could hear them scratching, chewing, moving, but no one else heard them. Just me. How strange that was.

With each step, I became more aware that I was abandoning the safety of the house. This was not something I would normally do. I did not venture outside of Pennbrook often, except for social calls. I wasn't adventurous like my brother Jameson or always out of doors like Jacob. To be honest, I only took walks in the garden when Claudette came to call. I did not like venturing out much. Yet, here I was running through the lawn in my nightgown in the middle of the night searching for my brother. The grass was wet under my feet, and my heart pounded so loudly I was certain that anyone near me would be able to hear it.

In a loud whisper, I called, "Jacob! Jacob! Where are you?"

The wind rose from the ground, and my loose hair and dress fluttered as I sailed across the lawn toward the woods. The pond was just beyond the smallish forest, and what was beyond that, I did not know.

"Jacob!" I whispered a little louder this time. The tall grasses around me spun like drunken dancers in a ballroom.

"Who is there?" I heard Jacob's frightened voice calling back to me from the line of woods just ahead.

"It's me, Mariana. Where are you?" I paused my flight as I scanned the tree line. Jacob's face rose up from the ground like a spirit rising from a grave. He waved at me and disappeared into the greenery.

With an exasperated sigh, I followed him and quickly caught up to him. Grabbing him by the shoulders, I turned him around. "What are you doing out here?

You can't be out here, Jacob. It is the middle of the night. Besides, you know the pond is off-limits. Is that where you are going?"

He shook his head slowly, his bottom lip poking out to express his displeasure with my interruption of his midnight adventure. "I was not going to the pond. I followed Jameson. He is out here hiding a treasure, and I want to find it." He fumbled with the button at the top of his nightdress and avoided looking me in the eye.

"Jacob, you do know those are not real treasures, don't you? Jameson isn't hiding gold or jewels. It's something else, nothing you want to see."

"I want to find it." Obviously, he was immovable in his determination.

"I have not seen anyone out here except you and me. It is the middle of the night, and tomorrow is my birthday party. We have to go back, Jacob. I think it might rain."

He narrowed his eyes. "Why do you lie to me? Just because I am young does not mean I am stupid. It is not going to rain, and I do not want to go inside until I find Jameson's treasure."

I glanced up and down the cluttered pathway. I saw no evidence that Jameson—or anyone else, for that matter—had passed this way. "Jacob, there is no one here. If Jameson hid a treasure, it would not be in these woods. You know how much he dislikes bugs of all kinds. And he would never hide his treasure so far from the house; he is smarter than that. You know that. I never said you were stupid, nor did I think it. Why don't we do this? We will go back to Pennbrook and look for the treasure on the way. But we must be very quiet. You know Jameson never wants us to know where he hides his treasures." Jacob smiled and put his arms around my waist. This was the first hug I had received from him in so long that I could not remember the last one.

The wind increased, and again my hair slapped my face. Jacob held my hand tight, and we walked back toward the house. I did not realize how far we had ventured out. True to my word, we paused every few feet to glance around for evidence of Jameson's recent excavations. I had no desire to pry into his personal business, but if it pleased Jacob and helped bring him back to the house, then I would certainly not discourage him from looking. I thought Jameson's treasures abhorrent; I wondered why Jacob would put so much value in them. And that worried me.

After the birthday party, once things returned to normal, for surely they would, I would speak to Father again about a governess. There must be someone willing to take my younger brother under their wing.

Someone besides Jameson.

I breathed a sigh of relief once we cleared the fountain even though the return trip was taking much longer than I expected. Together, we walked ever so slowly back to Pennbrook. Jacob insisted on looking under every rock, and that's when I saw him.

Jameson!

And he was not alone. My tall, gangly brother was wrapped in a woman's embrace. But whose? As they caressed and kissed, I watched and for a moment forgot that Jacob was there. I was shocked to see that Jameson was making love to Claudette. My hand flew to my mouth. Her hands rubbed his arms, and he held her tight and kissed her so deeply I thought surely he would devour her. Like two animals they were!

I heard Jacob's breath catch in his throat. I squatted down beside him and put my finger to my lips. He nodded in agreement but continued to stare at the unseemly display. The sickness that I'd felt earlier returned, but I could not succumb to it. We could not stay here and witness this any longer.

"Let's go to the front of the house, Jacob." He nodded again and held my hand tightly. We backed down the pathway and made a loop around to the front of the house. Once we turned the corner, we both ran; we were quite breathless as we stood on the porch. I squatted down again and said to him, "Say nothing to anyone about this. I will talk to Father, Jacob. You leave it to me, brother."

"But the treasure. We never found the treasure," he whined. I kissed his forehead and hugged him.

"I do not think the treasure is out here, anyway. I have never seen Jameson hide anything out here. Tomorrow when the sun comes up, you should go to the attic and look. I know he hides things up there. But do not let him find you searching. It will be worse for you if you do." He smiled and shook his head.

I forced myself to smile back. How was I going to tell Father about this?

Chapter Twelve—Jerica

As always, Jesse was the first one out of bed. If the sun was up, he was too; he didn't like sleeping in. I sure did, but with all the work we'd been doing, I wasn't afforded many opportunities. Still, I wasn't complaining. This was what I signed up for. At least I didn't hear the saw roaring this morning. Most of the woodworking had been completed; all that was left was the fine-tuning. Small things mostly, except for the installation of the plantation blinds. Yep, that was today. My arms weren't going to thank me. Those suckers were heavy to lift and hold.

After a few seconds of enjoying the quiet, I took a peek out the window just in time to see Jesse's truck driving down Hurlette. He'd be back soon with the shutters and window treatments. And Renee would be here too, if she wasn't already, as well as a few extra hands eager to finalize the renovations at Summerleigh and prepare for her official opening as a bed-and-breakfast.

There really wasn't much left to do, and that awareness brought a little sadness. *Why are you being so melancholy, Jerica?* It was as if the mood of Pennbrook had touched me in some strange way. Yes, I had Mariana on my mind. Why was the girl reaching out to me? I had no connection to her—not like Harper, who had been my close friend.

I heard a car horn honking in the distance. *No time for daydreaming, Jerica.* I had to get dressed so I could meet Jesse when he came back with the blinds. I looked forward to stretching my muscles and working with my hands, and I always slept better after a day of physical labor. As I headed off to my closet to retrieve today's uniform, blue jeans and a loose t-shirt, my eye caught a glint of something shiny. Was that gold? I walked over to Jesse's vacant pillow and picked up a thin necklace. *Hey, there's a pendant too!* I held the jewelry up to the light to admire it better. It was a dainty gold chain with a gold heart dangling from it. It was a choker style, and from the look of it, this was real gold. A present? From Jesse?

I smiled as I rubbed the smooth metal and turned it over in my hand. I gasped when I saw that there were initials engraved on it: MM.

Mariana McIntyre?

I looked around the room. No one had been in here, and if Jesse had mentioned anything about a necklace, I was sure I would have remembered it.

Maybe... No. Don't go there.

Jesse probably found this when he was digging around in the attic the other day. He wanted to surprise me is all. Yeah, that made sense. I put the necklace on and hovered in front of the mirror to examine how it looked on me. It was pretty, and I hoped Mariana would be happy I had it. I touched it one last time and then got dressed. Five minutes later, I tied my tennis shoes, pulled my hair up on top of my head and fired up the coffeepot. Toast would be my breakfast, that and some coffee. As I smeared cold butter on the toast, I reached for the phone.

Come on, Jerica. How impatient are you? You can wait a few minutes. He'll be back soon.

Instead of racing to the phone to ask Jesse about the necklace, I decided to be a grown-up and wait for the answers. I did a few more things around the house and then headed out with the keys in my hand. It was gorgeous out today. The sky was blue and clear with big, white puffy clouds. Not the kind of clouds that said, *Hey, I'm going to rain,* but the kind that made the sky appear as perfect as a picture. Yes, today had a dreamy kind of quality to it. A good dream, and I needed some of those after the strange hypnotic watching session I'd been having of Mariana and her family.

Jameson confused me. And Mariana's father should be ashamed of himself for being so distant, so unavailable. Did he intend to marry Claudette? I wondered how I could get more information. Surely there would be marriage records at the George County Courthouse? But maybe not. Jesse told me a couple of times that there was really no way of knowing much more about the McIntyre family since most of the historical data was missing.

I was surprised to see that Renee had beaten me to Summerleigh. She was so excited about stocking the pantry, and she chattered on and on. I listened patiently and helped her with the work. Apparently, there was a new restaurant opening in Lucedale right across the street from her diner. She was none too happy about it. Not too long after I arrived, Jesse reappeared with the promised load of blinds and some extra hands to help with them. Emanuel was there doing some work on the second floor installing canister lights in the former nursery. The wiring was giving him fits, as he put it, but he was determined to make it all work. I was glad to hear that. That room needed as many cheerful lights as we could give it. I shivered thinking of Marisol's bear hanging from the old fixture.

"Jerica, did you hear me? I said you are all booked up for November. Can you believe that, you guys? And there are three major events on the books and lots of excited locals who have already paid in advance—isn't that great?"

I nodded my head with a smile and said, "That is exciting news. I had no idea it would be so popular. I hope we can maintain the excitement."

"No second-guessing yourself, Jerica. Not having a change of heart, are you?" Renee's voice dropped, and she paused with her two cans of tomato sauce in her hands.

"Of course not. I'm not going anywhere. It's just that I've been thinking a lot about Mariana."

"The Lady in White? I haven't seen a thing, have you?"

"Not exactly, but I feel like there's something she's trying to tell me. Something about what happened to her. Everyone else has been found, and the truth is out about the Belle family secrets, but what about Mariana? Maybe she needs something too."

Renee twisted her lips and furrowed her brows thoughtfully. "I wouldn't be in too big of a hurry to solve every mystery, Jerica. Every old house needs a Lady in White, and you've got one. A real one. Look, you've done so much for Harper and those girls. You brought Jeopardy home. I mean, you've just done a lot already. Don't go putting yourself in danger again."

And for the first time today, I thought of Eddie. Shouldn't I be more afraid of the living than the dead? I'd heard that somewhere before. "I don't intend to, Ree-Ree."

"Sometimes we have all the answers we want; we can't always know everything that happened. Maybe Mariana just wants to be remembered by someone."

"Maybe." I couldn't believe Renee's attitude. What was she saying? What did she mean? That I should keep the Lady in White around like some kind of paranormal pet? I wasn't going to pay a bit of attention to that advice. I was going to find out what happened to Mariana. One way or another.

Jesse's handsome face appeared in the doorway. He pointed his power tool at me and said, "There's the girl I'm looking for. I could use your help with this. I brought Frank, but you know how handy he is. No offense, cousin."

She laughed at that. "None taken. I'll be the first to admit that Frank has two left feet and about ten thumbs. Y'all have fun. I'll catch the phone if it rings."

I followed Jesse to the front room, and we immediately began to unpack the first set of blinds. Fortunately for us, the shutter company had them all marked. "Hey, that's a nice necklace. I don't remember seeing that before," he said as the power drill whirred the screw into place.

"You left it for me. It was on your pillow." I elbowed him playfully as I toyed with the pendant.

He frowned. "No, I didn't."

My stomach felt like I was standing in an elevator that had decided to drop a few floors. "But I thought..." I dropped the pendant like it was on fire. "Okay. Then this is going to be really weird. Check this out." I held the pendant up for him to examine. He pushed his glasses up on his nose, and his eyes widened as he read the monogram.

"Does that say MM?"

"Some coincidence, huh?"

All of a sudden, Renee walked through with a basket of candles and picture frames. She got closer to see the pendant and said, "How lovely. Not to make myself look like an eavesdropper, but it sounds like The Lady in White left you a present." Jesse and I locked eyes as she walked through to the Great Room.

I dropped my voice and said, "And there's something else. I have to tell you about this photo that was in Harper's old room. It's of Addison's wedding day. I don't know how it got there because it wasn't there when I lay down. It's like both Harper and Mariana are trying to tell me something!"

Jesse had no chance to answer me because Renee popped back into the room. "Hey, I hate to interrupt, but there is a man here who wants to speak to the owner about possibly renting a room. He's in the kitchen."

I don't know why, but I stammered. Jesse said, "I'll go. Be right back."

I stopped him. "If you don't mind, let's call it a day. Round everyone up and head home, and we'll regroup tomorrow. There's some stuff going on, and I need to make sure it's safe for our guests before we open."

"Are you sure, Jerica? If you don't think it's safe, I should stay with you," Jesse said.

I put my hand on his chest and gave him a soft kiss. "I'm sure. I'll see you back at your place soon." I gave them a weak wave and headed up the stairs. I had to clear my head.

I had so much to think about. I had to figure this all out. Was this gift really from Mariana? Was she trying to tell me that she approved of what I was doing? That she wanted me to keep digging?

Nope. Nothing. I didn't have any answers.

All I knew was I had to find them.

Chapter Thirteen—Mariana

My birthday began like any other day, with the exception of the early arrivals at Pennbrook. A constant string of carriages rolled down the driveway, a precursor of tonight's festivities. I had expected to experience some anxiety at the prospect of my first official party as "the Lady of Pennbrook," but I was not prepared for this. And I'd had no idea I would spend this day without Claudette by my side.

However, I quickly realized the arrivals were here not to see me but rather to speak with my father. These men were his closest friends, or more to the truth, men of enterprise who had some business affiliation with Mr. Michael Bull McIntyre. Yes, Father obviously had some deal brewing in the pot, as he sometimes bragged, and these men were here for that purpose. They certainly wouldn't be here to see me. Would they?

The anxiety rose again, but I wasn't given much time to dwell on the meaning of it. Mrs. Tutwiler had managed to leave her son Donnie, who was faring better now after her ministrations. She'd been kind enough to come and set the house straight, oversee the arrangement of the decorations I had selected, and manage the food preparation. I had never been so happy to see the stern-faced woman. She appeared almost as excited as I was today. Her arrival lifted my mood; despite the machinations of my turncoat friend, it was going to be a joyous day.

Mrs. Tutwiler cooed over the magnolia swags I had cut and braided. I followed her around as she relocated them one by one, and I had to admit, her ideas were far more elegant than mine. She informed me in a whisper that Father had arranged for a three-piece ensemble to play a special concert in my honor at the beginning of the ball, and she assured me that every detail had been arranged. I felt very relieved to know that the weight of this celebration, of my own birthday, was not resting upon my incapable shoulders.

Claudette obviously did not come to my room as we had initially planned and thus was not there to fix my hair or help me prepare for the ball. Mrs. Tutwiler assisted me—I wanted to wear the new rose gown from my father, but she assured me that I should wait until later in the evening to put it on. This was my first ball, so I trusted her counsel. As she finished getting me ready, she said, "Your mother would be so proud to see this day. You have grown into a beautiful young woman, Mariana. Yes, she would be perfectly pleased with the sight of you."

With some surprise, I asked, "You knew my mother, Mrs. Tutwiler? Why have you never said so?"

Before we could continue our conversation, there was a knock at my door. A recognizably confident knock, not Claudette's soft tapping or Jameson's irritating series of pecks.

Mrs. Tutwiler hurried to the door to welcome my father. Mr. McIntyre was dressed in his best suit, his newest black one, along with a crisp white shirt with a black and silver bow tie. Father looked quite the picture, almost handsome. And he had gone to the trouble of waxing his mustache, too. I twirled about one more time as he showered me with compliments. Mrs. Tutwiler left us alone to talk about whatever it was he wanted to talk about.

And to think, I've been waiting since last night for this opportunity, and now it has presented itself to me. I will tell him everything! No one makes a fool out of Bull McIntyre! Or his daughter!

The door closed behind him, and I settled into my chair by the window and invited him to sit opposite me. "Thank you for my new dress, Father. It is the most beautiful thing I have ever owned. I look forward to wearing it later on. Thank you for the party and all the gifts. I can't believe how many people have arrived already."

"The Lotts are coming too. I want you to be kind to their son, Thaddeus. He is close to your age and an intelligent young man."

I promised to do so but couldn't worry about this request right now. I had much more pressing matters to discuss with him. Father smiled and slapped his knees as if that was all he had to say and he was ready to leave. I couldn't allow that. I had to tell him what I knew now before he could be embarrassed by it. And I was afraid that if I did not speak my mind now, I wouldn't have the courage to do so later. I just blurted it out, and as soon as the words came out of my mouth, I realized this may not have been the wisest course of action.

"I have to tell you something, Father. It concerns Claudette Paul—and Jameson." He tilted in his chair and surveyed me coolly. I swallowed and continued, "Last night, Jacob and I were outside. You know how he takes to wandering at all hours sometimes. We were coming back to the house, and I...I mean, we saw Claudette and Jameson. Together." I averted my eyes, unwilling to watch his anger erupt. Like so many said, Bull McIntyre was as unpredictable as they come if you got on his bad side. I never wanted to be on his bad side. I waited quietly, expecting a burst of angry, colorful language. But to my surprise, it never came. He remained quiet, controlled. He twisted the ends of his waxy mustache with his fingers and waited. Regret washed over me.

Why had I chosen to say this now? I rarely received visits such as this from my father, and to sully the moment with what he would surely consider gossip was a horrible idea. But as they say, in for a penny, in for a pound. I stammered on, "I do not believe that their meeting was altogether a holy meeting, sir. I thought you should know about it." I tilted my chin up now and looked him square in the eye. He didn't rage or scream or berate me. A low, dry laugh rolled out of his chest.

"And what would you know about holy meetings, Mariana? Are you insinuating that your brother and Miss Paul were behaving in an intimate manner? If you are going to make the accusation, you must be more specific. For you see, the arrangements have already been made. Unless you have seen them coupling or lying naked together, I cannot break my contract. Is that what you are saying? Speak plainly."

I blinked at his question. What was he asking me? Did he want details? I would not back down because I knew that what I had seen was not my imagination. They were not spirits in the moonlight. "I am sorry to hear that, but I did see them together. Ask Jacob if you do not wish to rely on my testimony alone. He saw it too. He was there. I swear it, Father." I felt the tears rise now, and my face flushed. This was getting worse by the minute. Not only did I have to tell my father bad news, but he did not believe me. "They were kissing one another and touching and doing other things, and Jacob–"

Father raised his hand and walked to the doorway. I could hear him asking Mrs. Tutwiler to bring Jacob to him. We sat in silence and waited for my brother to appear. Music was beginning to play downstairs; the musicians were tuning their instruments. I could hear laughter and lively talking; apparently, the libations were being served. My ruffles wilted around me, my neck felt sweaty, and my face was moist with tears. Yes, I intensely regretted telling him anything. Why had I done it? This was my party, and I had allowed Jameson to take the joy from my celebration. What was even worse was I knew my father did not believe me or did not want to believe me. I could not be sure which.

Jacob entered the room, and his big dark eyes shone with curiosity. He had been playing in the dirt; it was all over his knees. I surmised he'd been digging for Jameson's treasure somewhere outdoors. *He'll dig holes in the yard and blame it on Father's dogs.*

"Son, your sister says you were wandering last night. Is that true?"

Without missing a beat, he shook his head. "No, Father. But I have been outside all day today. I am about to get a bath and get ready for sister's party."

"Jacob, do not lie. Tell Father the truth. Tell him what we saw on the way back. Go on," I said as I gripped the sides of the chair desperately.

"I did not see anything, sister. I was asleep in my bed. Maybe you were dreaming?"

I jumped to my feet and blinked back tears. "You have to tell the truth, Jacob. Why are you lying? Is it to protect Jameson? You must see how this could hurt Father. Tell him what you saw!" I stamped my foot at him, but his innocent expression never wavered. He glanced fearfully at Father.

"You may go now, Jacob. Get your bath and come downstairs for the concert." Jacob walked to the door and gave me a cryptic look before he left the room.

"He is lying," I whispered.

Father walked to the window and peered down at the lawn below. He held his gold pocket watch in his hand, apparently to check the time. I knew that he had made up his mind not to believe me. "I am sure you are confused, Mariana. Maybe Jacob is right. You were dreaming."

"I wasn't dreaming," I said as I flopped back in my chair. "I was not dreaming, Father. I saw them together."

He didn't seem to hear me. "You have heard by now that I intend to marry Claudette. I wish that whoever had told you would have done me the courtesy of allowing me to share this news with you, but I can see that the servants have been gossiping again. Or was it Mrs. Tutwiler?"

"No, Father. Mrs. Tutwiler has not been gossiping." I felt all my joy vanish in that moment, and I wiped at my tears with the back of my hand.

"Good. I know that the idea of my marrying again seems strange to you, as I have been a bachelor for so long, but it is my intent to do so. Judge Paul has agreed to the union, and as you and Claudette are friends, I believed you would be happy to have her so close by. Whatever disagreement you have with your friend, you must settle it—because she will be my wife, Mariana." He wiped my face with his handkerchief and handed it to me. "Keep it, but I want those tears gone when you come down the stairs."

"Yes, Father."

"Time to put those childish ideas away now. No petty jealousy between you and Claudette or your brother. We will be a family." He popped open his pocket watch one last time and snapped it shut.

"From this day forward, you must behave like an adult. I have been patient with you, Mariana, but it is time to move on. You cannot grieve for your mother all your life; you never even knew her. There is so much you don't know." He walked to the door and stared at it, his back to me. He was struggling with the idea of telling me something but, unlike me, decided against it. "Finish getting ready for your party, and no more idle talk." He left my room without another word to me. And I could think of nothing else to say to him.

I had told him the worst, and he did not believe me. I was no fortune-teller, but I could see the future in that moment.

Horrible things were about to happen.

Chapter Fourteen—Jerica

For the first time, the nursery felt warm and peaceful. Almost welcoming. At least that's what I told myself. Tucking myself into an overstuffed seat, I rubbed my hand over the soft throw blanket. We had decided that this would become the upstairs parlor, a kind of bonus room for guests staying on the top floor. None of the ghosts of yesterday could touch the beauty of this space now. What a great idea to go with this lively blue and taupe color combination. It was the most contemporary-looking room in the house, the complete opposite of what it used to look like. And that was due in no small part to Renee, who had proved to be invaluable in the renovation and decoration process. She'd managed to completely change the room, no more dark foreboding shades of deep burgundy and hunter green covering the walls. I sighed, the warmth disappearing from the room—and my bones. This room had been such an unhappy place, and no amount of paint and throw blankets and candles would change that.

Not anymore. That can't be true. Not anymore.

Even as I thought the words, I did not believe them. Nope. As much as I pretended otherwise, the nursery still played an unhappy note, a mournful strum that hummed beneath everything else. No, this place did not want to be happy.

"Well, it's going to be," I said to no one in particular. And that's when I heard the notes, soft and sweet at first and then more frantic. *Oh yes, this was a familiar sound. Was that a piano? Yes, it was a piano!*

I sat up on the settee and moved the pillows to the side. I heard nothing, but then the music returned, only louder, more present. Yes! There it was again. The sound of the piano! But we had no piano. I had to investigate this noise immediately. Jesse and I had talked about installing a stereo system but had not taken steps to do so. Not yet. Was this a CD player? It couldn't be; the sound was too close, too full, like there was a recital taking place downstairs. I walked to the open door and poked my head into the hallway. I suspected that as soon as I stepped into the hallway the sound would disappear, but it didn't. Now, I heard the piano playing even more loudly. I swallowed and checked the other rooms. All the doors were closed. I checked every room, but there wasn't a soul in the place, no CD player and certainly not a grand piano.

"Renee? Jesse? Are you still here? Anyone?"

No one answered, and I swore silently under my breath. I wasn't one to swear much and didn't do it well, but this was definitely a swear-word moment. Why had I sent everyone home? I was beyond goose bumps, and my hands and arms felt icy cold. Instinctively, I rubbed them to try to warm myself back up. Out of the blue, a stabbing pain in my stomach struck me so hard that it made me bow forward slightly. I clutched my gut in surprise and felt a wave of nausea hit me.

"Oh God," I whimpered as I gripped the nearby doorframe. I waited for the pain to pass and then flicked off the light and closed the door behind me as I headed to the stairs. The piano notes became softer, the music calmer; it was a familiar tune. Was that Chopin? It was certainly not Mozart. I racked my brain trying to remember, trying to recall those long-ago days in my Music Appreciation class. Back then I would've known who I was listening to. Then it dawned on me. Beethoven! That was it! Beethoven's Moonlight Sonata.

As I put my foot on the top of the stairs, the music stopped and I heard the moving of furniture, as if someone had hurriedly pushed back the piano bench. But again I had to remind myself that there was no piano here and no piano bench. I hurried to the bottom landing and stood there, steeling my nerves to make the final few steps into the Great Room. Once more, the pain twisted in my stomach. I leaned against the wall gasping for breath between spasms.

When I could finally breathe normally, I called, "Jesse?" I hoped he would answer me, that someone would answer me, but I knew I was alone. My hand went to my stomach, and I half expected to pull it away and see blood there, so deep and painful was this sensation. I closed my eyes as they watered and waited for the pain to pass. As the pain loosened its hold on me, I waited. A board creaked below.

Probably the house settling. That's all. Just the house settling. Please be that.

A familiar voice echoed from the Great Room. "Hello, Jerica. I have been waiting for you. Impatiently waiting." With heavy legs and even heavier footsteps, I walked down the last few stairs and stepped into the Great Room. The custom-made furniture had arrived earlier, and the place was beautifully accommodated, ready for guests. But this visitor was certainly unwanted and unwelcome.

How did he get in here? Had I left the door unlocked? I couldn't have. I never do!

Eddie Poole sat in one of the chairs near the large picture window. His bony arms were crossed as if he were some sort of demented physician waiting to diagnose his patient.

"Please, Jerica. Dear wife, come and join us."

I stepped closer. "Us? Who are you talking about, Eddie?"

I had another visitor, who manifested like an inky portrait image being developed right before my eyes. She sat like an old-fashioned wooden doll in the chair beside Eddie. I watched her touch my ex-husband's hand as if they were the greatest of friends. The closest. The most intimate. I couldn't believe what I was seeing.

I was looking at the ghost of Claudette Paul.

Chapter Fifteen—Jerica

The deep, stabbing pain returned, and my knees buckled. *No, please. Don't do this now. What is happening to me?* My nurse's brain worked on a diagnosis, but the agonizing ache was like nothing I could describe. I had to be hallucinating. That couldn't really be Claudette Paul.

"What are you doing here?"

"I think you know why I am here. I was invited, dear wife. I am here to collect on a debt that I am owed."

I put my hand up to fend him off as he walked toward me slowly. Eddie behaved like a man impaired, under the influence of some sort of narcotic. But he was clearing the distance between us rather quickly, and panic rose within me.

"What debt? You have to get out of here. Get out of my house, Eddie!" I yelled as the pain increased. "Leave before the police arrive. I have this place wired. They'll know you are here."

Eddie walked up beside me and stared down at me, and he seemed to enjoy my pain because I heard him laughing. "By the time they arrive, I will have collected my debt and then it won't matter. Will it?" He chuckled, and it was a low, horrible sound. How was Claudette involved in all this? Was it she who had summoned Eddie here? Or was it just his pure hatred for me, his absolute disgust for me, that led him to Summerleigh?

Whatever the answer, I knew I was in trouble. Why had I told Jesse to go home? He had wanted to stay, but I had to push myself. I had to be here at Summerleigh by myself. I had to visit the nursery just one more time. Check it out, just to make sure everything was safe. But it wasn't safe. Not at all. And now I'd made a horrible mistake.

I had my cell phone in my pocket, and that gave me hope. If I could get to it, I could call for help. But right now, I had to focus on getting to my feet.

Harper! If you can hear me—I'm in trouble!

Finally, the pain lifted, but Eddie had me by the back of my hair. He dragged me to my feet as I screamed, more in anger than in pain. "Stop, you bastard!"

"Oh, nice. So classy, Nurse Jerica. Is that any way to talk to your husband?"

With a twist of my upper body, I lifted my foot and kicked backward, hitting him in the leg. It wasn't enough to take him down, but it freed me from his grasp. *No way! I wasn't going to die alone at the hands of Eddie Poole!* I backed away from Eddie but didn't dare make a fast move, and I sure didn't risk pulling out my phone. Not yet. I had to make a run for it first, but I needed more time.

You know how to do this, Jerica. You were a counselor and a nurse, for Pete's sake. You can do this. Focus on the patient.

"Okay, Eddie. I know that you are hurting, but you have to explain to me why you are here. Tell me, what do you want? What can I help you with?"

And then I had the opportunity to look him fully in the face. This man was a shadow of the man I once loved; I had loved him so deeply that I had been willing to do anything for him. His long, narrow nose looked so out of place in his face. Had he broken it recently? Yes, it was crooked. There was no trace left of the man I had loved. He'd shaved off his hair, and I could see scars on his hands, face and arms. For an instant, I felt sympathy for him until I saw what was in his right hand.

Eddie was holding a pair of silver shears.

"Eddie, put those scissors down. You don't need those to talk to me. I think we can work this out if you..."

And then to my complete surprise, Eddie swung the shears in front of him like a child swinging at a piñata. But this was nothing as pleasant as that. He wanted to cut me, to kill me, to make me bleed. And now, a few feet behind him, Claudette was moving closer. She appeared washed out like a black-and-white picture, and she wore a raggedy ball gown. Claudette looked like an awful creature. Her dead eyes were ringed with black shadows, her white lips moved, and she wore a hungry expression as if she would love nothing more than to devour me. She was speaking but not to me—she was whispering to Eddie.

I screamed as I tumbled backwards, tripping over my own two feet, but I quickly regained my footing. I sprinted around the couch to escape them, but I didn't make the mistake of trying to run any further. Claudette's image flickered out and reappeared near the front door, as if she knew I was going to try to escape. Eddie growled like an animal next to me, and he began to sob as he waved the shears again. He waved them wildly like some sort of macabre puppet under the control of an invisible, devilish puppeteer.

"You killed my daughter! I knew you hated me; I knew you were going to leave me. You planned the whole thing, didn't you? I thought you might try to take Marisol from me, but you murdered her instead. Why, Jerica? Why? You merciless bitch! You took everything from me."

I sobbed at the accusation. He believed it—he really believed it! "Eddie, I wasn't leaving you. I never even considered that. I loved you, and that is not what happened. How dare you believe that I would harm Marisol? I loved her! I loved you! I am sorry. If I could take it back, I would. Don't you think I wished it was me that died and not her?"

As if to answer my question, he plunged the shears into the couch nearest me, his hateful glare focused on me. With all his rage, he stabbed the couch again and again. I should have run, but I was stunned by his savagery and could do nothing but watch.

"You are a liar, Jerica. A murdering liar!"

Remember, stay focused. Talk to him. All you need is ten seconds to get to that door.

"I don't know what's going on with you, Eddie, but it's not too late. If you are sick, and you must be, I can help you. You are delusional if you believe that I would hurt our daughter!" I replied to him as calmly as possible. Yes, I had to be calm. Being calm would help him. The police should arrive soon. The alarm system had been active, or so I hoped. Surely they would arrive any minute now.

"Eddie you shouldn't have come here. There are spirits here that influence people who are sick. You are sick, Eddie. You need a doctor, and I can help you find one. You know I can. Remember that time your appendix burst? I was there. And that time you wrecked out on your motorcycle? I was there every minute. I loved you, Eddie."

I continued to move to my left around the back of the chaise, and I couldn't stop the tears from coming. I didn't want to cry, but I also didn't want to die. It didn't appear that I would be able to get to the front door, but there was an alternate exit in Ann's bedroom. If I could just get there.

That's what I would do. I would make my move and run down that hallway. The kitchen would be too far, but this way...I could make this run.

And then the lamp crashed to the floor. Eddie struck it down with his hand, and I jumped at the sound of the breaking pottery.

"Don't talk to me, Jerica, and don't speak her name. You are not worthy of her! And you were never worthy of her, you crazy—" Before he could finish his slur, footsteps banged across the ceiling above us. *Someone else was here.* "Is your friend hanging around? Isn't he man enough to come face me? Hey! Come down here, you punk! I've got something for you too!" He was distracted, or so I thought, so I tossed a glance at the door that led to the hallway. The footsteps continued, louder now, as if someone in heavy boots were stomping around. Those weren't high heels clicking on the wood but the boots of a soldier. Then the floor shook and the chandelier began to swing.

Immediately, I saw Claudette's image change. Her face morphed into one of terror, and she wavered as if she were an image on an old television screen that flickered in and out. And just like that, she vanished. Eddie's eyes widened; I saw confusion and terror there. Was it possible that the spirit's hold on him, the evil influence of Claudette Paul, had been broken or at least weakened?

"Eddie, we have to leave this place. You have to stop this. This is madness!"

He was crying now but still had the scissors in his hand. "My daughter! You killed her, Jerica. You took her from me." He continued to cry and swear, and now he was waving the shears in great arcs as he came toward me. I could run to the front door now if I wanted to, and I might be able to make it. But maybe not. Even as I glanced in that direction, his eyes followed me. His pale lips were cracked and covered with sores. As he snarled at me, I could clearly see his broken teeth. Oh, how could I have loved this man? This couldn't be my ex-husband. This creature was nothing but a disgusting doppelgänger of Eddie Poole.

"You aren't going anywhere, Jeri girl. You are gonna pay for what you did to my daughter. She was the only good thing left for me. The last of my soul, Jerica. She was the last of my soul."

"No, Eddie. You are still in there. You can still have a life. Marisol would want you to live, and you know I would never harm her. I loved her as much as I loved you."

"I told you not to say her name! You'll pay for that!" The gaunt skeleton of a man launched himself toward me. *I have to make my move now! No more stalling!*

I pushed the armchair over as hard as I could. It wouldn't stop him for long, but maybe it would slow him down. I raced toward the hallway that would lead me to the bedroom hallway. I slammed the door with a scream of anger, wishing it had a lock. I ran as fast as I could, but the pain in my stomach returned and seized me again. I flung myself against the wall opposite Harper's bedroom. I couldn't speak or breathe; all I could do was lean against the wall and wait for the pain to subside.

What is going on? What's wrong with me?

Eddie slung the door open, and I crept away as far as I could until the pain was so great that I collapsed on the floor. He laughed as he walked toward me. And here I would die. Here in the hallway at Summerleigh, so close to Harper. So many had died here—why not one more?

Although my stomach pain intensified, I dragged myself away with both my hands. Surely this pain would only last a few more seconds, just like before. If I could wait it out, I could get away. I still had a chance.

I crawled a few inches, but then Eddie was next to me. I could see the scissors in his hand. They were old scissors, antiques, really. They were severely rusted, or was that dried blood? I could hardly tell.

"Eddie... Don't do this."

I expected him to say something cruel, to taunt me as he did his horrible deed, but that didn't happen. I heard a door squeaking and shoes walking toward us. Then I could see the shoes. Whoever she was, she wore old-fashioned saddle shoes, the black-and-white ones. I couldn't look up as pain held me in its grip, but I knew by the bobby socks and shoes who it was that approached. Was this Harper come at last to collect me since I was about to die?

"Harper," I whispered. And then I heard Eddie scream. I realized that I could move again and that the pain had lifted.

"Harper?" I screamed as I ran down the hall. I wanted to look back, to see her one last time, but I wanted to live even more. I propelled myself down the hall on wobbly legs until I reached Ann's bedroom. I opened the door and practically slung myself over the bed. I raced to the side door, but it was locked. I could hear Eddie screaming and running after me. He called me foul names again and again, but I wasn't listening to him. I could hear a second pair of shoes slapping on the floor.

Finally, the door opened for me and I tumbled out onto the porch. *Oh God, this hurts! Had I twisted my ankle on top of everything else?* The door slammed behind me, and I heard Eddie swearing again. A great crashing sound echoed in the bedroom behind the closed door, as if someone had knocked the dresser over and moved the bed around. I heard Eddie's frightened cry once more. I crawled off the stairs into the yard and finally dug into my pocket for my cell phone. Eddie's screams continued, and my hands shook with fear. How long could Harper keep him there? I wasn't sure. I don't know why I didn't call the police, but I couldn't think straight. I dialed Jesse's number.

"Jesse? I need you to come to the house. Eddie is here. Please!" And then the stabbing sensation hit me again, and this time the pain was so great that I felt a great tide of blackness wash over me.

When my eyes fluttered open, I could see the face of a young woman in front of me. I knew this face. This was Mariana McIntyre.

Mariana, I see you. Am I dead?

A peaceful smile stretched across her face, and I felt her cool hand touch my cheek. And then she was gone. She was no longer there; I was looking into the face of someone I had never seen before.

"Ma'am? Can you hear me?"

"Yes. I can hear you. Am I dead?"

The woman in the nurse's uniform shook her head. "No, but you are one lucky woman. You had an ulcer, but you're on the mend. I think you have a visitor if you're up to seeing him."

"What? I'm in the hospital?"

"Yes, ma'am. You've been here a few days. You are going to be alright now, Mrs. Poole."

"It's Jerica. I'm Jerica Jernigan," I said with all the strength I could muster.

I heard another voice beside me, a familiar voice and one that I wanted to hear with all my heart.

"Look who is awake. I thought...I'm glad to see you, Jerica."

"Me too, Jesse. I'm glad to see you too." And then I felt so tired, so very tired. I had to close my eyes for a few minutes. Just a few. "Don't leave, okay?"

"Never. I'm never leaving again."

I started to say, "Thank you," or "I love you," but the words didn't come.

I fell into a place beyond sleep.

Chapter Sixteen—Mariana

The striking pianist's fingers moved over the ivory keys so effortlessly that it seemed like a bit of magic to watch him play. Thaddeus Lott, as he was introduced to us by my father, leaned into Beethoven's Moonlight Sonata as he closed his eyes. This selection always made me weep, but tonight no tears came for I could not take my eyes off the young man's face. It was certainly a handsome face; many other young women in the room obviously agreed. It was angular, elegant and illuminated by candlelight. His pink lips moved slightly as he allowed the music to carry him to faraway places. I traveled with him. Dark-fringed eyes stared into the darkness beyond the conservatory windows, and then they were watching me, but only for a second. He did not leer at me. However, I could not take my eyes off of him.

Oh! He caught me staring, and I believed I saw the hint of a smile tug at the corners of his mouth. But then it disappeared, like the music that vanished into the night air. Suddenly, my gown felt as if it tightened around me; I was short of breath and reminded myself to breathe evenly.

Keep your composure, Mariana.

Someone was watching me; the hair began to prickle on the back of my neck. Angry to be torn away from Mr. Lott's musical performance, I glanced sternly in Claudette's direction. She smiled at me politely, but I gave her no hope of being forgiven. *She may fool my father, but she will not make a fool of me. Never again.* And then suddenly Thaddeus Lott's music recaptured my attention as it intensified, the notes precise and persistent. I felt the audience's collective breath catch as he picked at the notes like a madman. A handsome, wonderfully talented madman. The lady beside me, whose name escaped me, began to frantically fan herself as if the speed of the music had raised her temperature. I smiled at the idea but kept my eyes on Mr. Lott.

Father had asked me to befriend him; I suddenly became very open to the idea of a friendship with this talented musician. *In this I shall be obedient, but I will certainly wait for Father to make my introductions.* It would hardly be proper to extend my hand to him without first being formally introduced. Would this piece never end? I wanted to meet this young man, talk with him and maybe even dance with him. The ballroom would be ready now; I could not wait to see it. Suddenly, Claudette sat beside me. Her posture was perfect, her face the picture of grace and beauty, but I could sense her worry. She knew that I knew. She'd figured it out. I wondered if Father mentioned it to her. I moved my skirt a few inches to avoid touching hers as if she would contaminate me.

"Sister," she whispered without leaning too far in my direction, "I must talk to you."

"Must you?" I whispered back and shifted in my chair. It would be the height of rudeness to walk out on my guest's performance, so I would not, but I did not believe I had to endure chitchat with my former friend.

"Mariana," she began in a low whisper.

"Please, be quiet," I hissed as I turned my full attention back to Thaddeus Lott, and as quick as that, the sonata ended and the applause began. I eagerly applauded too as he stood to graciously accept our praise for his beautiful performance.

Father stepped into the aisle and offered his hand to me. Claudette rose too and smiled in an overly friendly manner. Without frowning at her—and that was a tremendous feat—I accepted his hand and we began to greet those who had gathered to celebrate my birthday. I knew many of the faces although some names escaped me. Even after introductions, I was unable to remember all their names. But Thaddeus Lott and his father, George Lott, I would always remember. Two more handsome faces I had never seen.

"Please allow me to introduce my daughter, Mariana, and her friend, Claudette Paul. Ladies, this young man is Thaddeus Lott. And this is his father, George Lott."

"Ladies, we are honored to meet you both." Thaddeus bowed slightly to the two of us but barely glanced in Claudette's direction. I liked him even more. Jameson passed by behind Thaddeus but did not dare intrude.

"Thank you for playing, Mr. Lott. I wish I could play the piano with such precision, but alas, I have two hands with ten thumbs."

"Do not pretend that you are not talented, Mariana. You have the voice of an angel," Claudette purred with faux sincerity.

"Whatever my other skills might be, I could never play the piano so beautifully as my mother did. They say musical talent skips a generation. Many people say my mother was such a moving pianist that people wept when they heard her play. But alas, as I said, I have no such talent." My father's dark eyes pierced mine as I realized he was very unhappy with me. Yes, I had pushed him too far. Claudette frowned too, but both our guests were oblivious to the tension.

The younger Lott's lips curled and revealed two dimples, one in each cheek. "I hear there is a cure for that," he said in a warm, friendly voice.

"What would that be?" I asked curiously, happy to be in conversation with this beautiful young man.

"Practice," he said. My heart sank at his reply, but he obviously did not mean to insult for he followed up his comment quickly with a surprising offer. "Perhaps you need a better teacher. I would of course be happy to offer my services. Music is my passion, Miss McIntyre."

"Oh, yes. I would like that."

The five of us stood awkwardly for a few seconds until Thaddeus said, "If I may be so bold, Miss McIntyre, I wonder if you would dance with me. Your father has mentioned that you enjoy the waltz. I do as well, but I fear I am not a skilled dancer."

I smiled and answered, "I hear there is a cure for that, Mr. Lott." Everyone laughed except my father, who merely watched the exchange. Was I being too flirtatious? I had no time to wonder, for the ballroom doors slid open and the violins began to soar. I could not hide my delight. Mrs. Tutwiler had exceeded my expectations—the place looked like a scene from heaven. Gold-toned candlesticks held white candles, and green and white ribbons hung from the curtains that were elegantly pulled back from the massive windows. I felt that I was indeed the Lady of Pennbrook tonight.

As if she read my mind, Claudette came to my side, but I turned away only to walk into Jameson. He would not budge but stared down at me rudely. I nudged him in the chest with my elbow and swirled around him as he tugged at one of my ribbons. I could see a gleam of devilish delight in his eye. My brother would love nothing more than to cut off all my hair and strip every ribbon from my gown, but my rescuer, Thaddeus Lott, remained close and said smoothly, "Miss McIntyre, how about this dance? It is a waltz, and I am anxious to make your further acquaintance."

"Thank you, Mr. Lott. I would be delighted," I replied, trying not to smile too broadly or speak too hurriedly.

"Please call me Thaddeus," he said as he offered his hand. I put my gloved hand on top of his and ignored the whispers.

"Very well, Thaddeus. You may call me Mariana."

"Mariana. What a musical name."

For the next hour, I sailed around the ballroom with various guests, but none pleased me as much as Thaddeus Lott. As we laughed and enjoyed one another's company, I decided then and there that I would behave. I would not tempt Father's anger again as he had arranged this new friendship and clearly, he and Mr. Lott hoped a deeper friendship would bloom between Thaddeus and me.

Soon, the ensemble rose and received their prize, our applause and admiration. The ballroom had grown warm, the faces of the cheerful attendees were pink, and many folks headed for the porches and the gardens beyond. Confused, I asked Mrs. Tutwiler what was happening.

"Oh, my dear, I forget how young you are sometimes. This is the intermission. It will last for an hour, and then there will be another hour of dancing. During the intermission, the men will take cigars and bourbon in Mr. McIntyre's study."

"What will the ladies do, Mrs. Tutwiler?" I felt ashamed that I did not know, but I was grateful to have her insight.

"Why, they will tidy themselves, tend to their hair, their gowns, whatever they like. But you can be sure many will be talking about you and that young Mr. Lott." She patted my hand and led me up the stairs. "In my time, the ladies took naps, but that was for afternoon balls. As you are the hostess of the party, you have the upper hand. You could change your gown if you like and then return to the ball looking fresh and beautiful while your guests will look a bit wilted. It is after all your birthday."

My eyes lit up as realization dawned. "Oh! Is that why you told me not to wear my new gown yet?"

"You are a very bright young woman," Mrs. Tutwiler said with a smile. She rarely smiled, and I hugged her to thank her. She patted my back and kissed my cheek. Another first for me. "Your father has thought of everything, Mariana. And Thaddeus Lott—you approve of him, obviously."

"How generous Father is to me! I cannot believe he would be so kind. I should go apologize; I have hurt him, Mrs. Tutwiler. I really should." I pulled my gloves off and chewed my nail until Mrs. Tutwiler fussed at me.

"He is busy at the moment making arrangements for his own happiness. You can talk to him later, Mariana. Now come on, let's go get you changed."

What could that mean?

Just then, a housemaid interrupted, "Excuse me, Mrs. Tutwiler? Jacob needs you. He's very sick and has thrown up all over himself. I don't know what to do, ma'am." The girl appeared sick herself and certainly not capable of taking care of Jacob. Yes, we needed a governess. Then I had an idea, what if Mrs. Tutwiler became Jacob's governess? She knew how to take care of the house. She had one of her own. But why would she do such a thing when she had Oak Lawn to run? Her husband died five years ago, but the house was her family home.

"Go ahead, Mrs. Tutwiler. I can get one of the house servants to help me. I will come down soon."

She left me alone in the hallway. There were people everywhere, including Claudette who stared at me with fierce determination. I immediately spun on my heel and went into my room and closed the door.

I sat on the bed, but Claudette did not knock. I waited another few minutes and heard nothing at all except for the voices of other excited young women in the hallway. I imagined I heard my name on their lips.

Yes, Thaddeus and I would be the talk of the town by now, or at least the talk of Pennbrook. With furious fingers, I began to tug at the ribbons that had me bound. No. It was no good. Mrs. Tutwiler had knotted one or two of them. I would need an extra pair of hands. As I walked to the door to call for a servant, a voice behind me surprised me.

"Please, sister. Allow me to help you with that."

I spun around to see Jameson, and as quick as lightning, his hand wrapped around my throat.

Chapter Seventeen—Mariana

"What do you think you know, sister? I know so much more than you do. I always have. I know about our mother. Fever didn't take her. Sickness didn't claim her. It was Father who did her in."

My throat hurt so badly, I could barely breathe, and I was so frightened I believed I might die. "Jameson, st-op," I gurgled as he continued to apply pressure to my throat.

"Say, 'You know more, Jameson'. Say it!" Jameson's voice was flat, and his face was the picture of hatred. And it was me that he hated—his own sister. Partially releasing my neck, he said in a near growl, "Say it!"

"Jame-son...please stop." He squeezed me again, and I gasped for breath and my eyes watered. *Would he kill me on my birthday?*

"Say that I know more than you or I will put you to sleep, Mariana. You could go to sleep and never wake up. Just like Mother." He leaned over me, his face just an inch from mine. The weight of his body forced me down into the mattress, and I began to cry silently. *I will die! I will die tonight! Any second!*

But the bedroom door opened and to my surprise, Claudette walked inside. She closed the door behind her and immediately I knew I was doomed. She did not come to my aid or try to stop Jameson from performing his evil task.

They were going to kill me to keep their secret. *But it wasn't a secret anymore. I told Father, only he didn't believe me!* I saw spots form before my eyes. I saw bright lights, and then everything went black. I was dying. I had to be dying. One would die if one could not breathe. My lungs burned, my eyes ached, and I passed out.

Or maybe I died.

No. That's not right. I'm awake now.

I was in my bed, finally wearing my new gown. But I could barely move. Jameson had left us, but my former companion Claudette remained. I noticed that she held a pair of silver shears. I wanted to speak, but I could not, not yet. My throat hurt, and my heart beat rather slowly. I wasn't sure I was still alive. Maybe I was dead...*yes, please let me be dead.*

"I know you cannot talk to me, Mariana. You cannot speak because Jameson crushed your windpipe. That is unfortunate, because I would like to hear your apology. Why did you have to ruin everything? Why? You should not have spied on me, Mariana. You should have left well enough alone. For you see, I am going to be the Lady of Pennbrook now. You should have accepted me, accept that I do not love your father, that I love Jameson. Your father is a killer. Would you rather he kill me too?"

I tried to speak but only hissed. She smiled as she clipped at my hair. She held up a lock of it to me and then tossed it on the floor beside the bed. "Jameson and I love one another, Mariana. And we understand one another. You cannot spoil it, although this pains me, you just cannot. But now, I am going to claim a souvenir first. Just a few to remember you by when you have gone. Yes, I am afraid you must die, sweet Mariana, but do not worry your pretty head about it. I will make sure you are buried with all the respect due you, and as your father's wife, I will mourn you immensely."

Suddenly, I began to scream, but nothing came out of my mouth. Not a sound, just an empty scream. I called for Father, Mrs. Tutwiler and Jacob, but no one heard me. Not even the people in the hallway outside could hear me. But I could hear them. Life was so close! Thaddeus was so close!

"What a lovely new dress, Mariana, dear. So lovely. The perfect dress to die in."

I squirmed away from her, but she was on me like a hungry cat on a fat mouse that had been foolish enough to give away his position.

And I was murdered as quickly as that.

Horrible, gut-wrenching pain pierced me, accompanied by hot warmth on my skin and then coldness in my body. The cold was so fierce and chilled my soul. I did not feel anything after the first stab. She stabbed me a second time and then rose from the bed to watch me bleed. I stared at the horrible smile on her face. That's when I saw him. My little brother was hiding beneath the table and no one had seen him. He'd seen the whole thing. I wanted to tell him to run, to go tell Father, but I felt dizzy, like I was falling down the staircase. Or like my soul was falling out of my body.

I died so quickly. I died too soon.

I never kissed Thaddeus as I had hoped to.

I hovered near my body...waiting for what, I didn't know. And another door opened; it had been a part of the wall. I never knew that was there! Jameson stepped back into the room, and although I could not hear them, I could see that he was angry. Angry with Claudette! She pleaded with him about something, but what? I could not hear, and the room was growing dark now.

And then I heard Father's voice. Father's voice calling me, his fist banging on the door.

Finally, the door was open and I saw him, his face broken in tears as he witnessed my bloody end.

And then everything changed.

I could no longer see my father. I was in another place. No, wait. This place was so like home but not quite. The color had faded from my new dress, my face and everything about me. I walked up and down the halls looking for Jacob. Poor, frightened Jacob. I did not hate him. He could never have saved me. I worried for him, hoped he would love. I had to show him that I was alive.

And then I found another child. A little girl with golden hair; she wore it in two braids. We talked often. Her name was Loxley. She lived here now, but this was no longer Pennbrook.

This was her house. This was Summerleigh.

And I was the Lady in White.

Epilogue—Jerica

With only thirty minutes to kill before my drive to Mobile, I felt antsy this morning. This was a recent development but not an entirely unwelcome one. In the past, this kind of anxiety often preceded a supernatural encounter.

No, I didn't feel afraid. I was excited by the prospect of seeing someone I loved. Would I see Harper? Maybe Jeopardy? I couldn't guess what was about to take place, but I felt compelled to go for a walk. And even as my feet stepped onto the familiar pathway, I knew my destination.

The potting shed.

I zipped up my jacket and waved goodbye to Renee, who was busy preparing for a new infusion of weekend guests. How could I manage all this without her? I hoped I never had to know. One day soon, very soon, she would be my cousin-in-law, if that was a real thing. Closing the door behind me, I shoved my hands in my plaid jacket pockets.

Only thirty minutes to kill, Jerica. You can't miss a minute of Jesse's big day.

And I wouldn't dream of it. Jesse's latest book, *The Ghosts of Pennbrook*, was a regional hit, and his publisher was very excited about his future. I remembered the night he typed THE END. We celebrated with a kiss, a little champagne and a completely wonderful marriage proposal.

And this time I said, "Yes!" without hesitation.

"But I want to do it quickly," I told him.

"Afraid you'll change your mind?" he asked while he posed in his signature power move, leaning back against the couch with his arms crossed.

"I'm not changing my mind, Jesse. My only concern is my dress." I slid my arms around his narrow waist and smiled coyly.

He gave a low and sexy laugh and kissed me, his relief obvious. As if I wouldn't want to marry him. "Jerica, I am sure any dress you choose will be perfect. Just like you."

"Thank you for the compliment, but we both know I'm not perfect." I kissed him back. "It's not my style selection I'm worried about. It's the fit." A dark strand of hair fell into my eyes, and Jesse tucked it behind my ear as he always did. I blushed thinking about his voice purring in my ear earlier during an intimate session.

I always want to see your beautiful eyes, Jerica.

I tried not to chuckle at his confusion now. "You lost me, honey."

Still smiling up at him, I rubbed my stomach and held it protectively. "I don't want to waddle down the aisle, Jesse. So sooner rather than later, please."

"What?" His puzzled expression made me laugh out loud. Then realization dawned on his handsome face. "You mean...we..."

"You are going to be a daddy, Jesse Clarke." And to my surprise, he cried. He held me and cried. And I couldn't have loved him any more than I did at that moment.

"When?"

"Let's see. It's December now, and I'm three months...so June, I think. At least that's what the doctor says, but it's subject to change by a week or two."

"What do we do now? I mean, is there anything I can do?"

I laughed again. "I think your contribution to this process is over for now. But thanks for the support." We hugged and laughed and cried some more. Yes, it was a wonderful moment.

A little more than a year had passed since we'd solved the mystery of Mariana McIntyre. And to think, Hannah had even gotten it wrong. Jameson had not murdered his sister—Claudette committed that heinous crime. But now the world knew the truth, thanks to Jesse's hard work. He gave me credit in his book for my part, but I didn't really care about that. The ghosts had been put to rest, and all was well here at Summerleigh. If a little lonely.

I was glad everyone was at peace. Except with the way I was feeling, that may not be true. Someone was waiting for me! *Just a quick walk, Jerica. Get moving. If you miss your fiancé's book signing, you'll never hear the end of it.* The gravel crunched underneath my boots, and I flipped the jacket collar up to shield my bare neck from the growing cold. Why had I worn a ponytail today? A few brown leaves fluttered to the ground, the last remnants of fall. Suddenly, I paused as I heard a sound. A familiar sound, like a shovel digging in the dirt. I hadn't hired a gardener yet, so who could be out here digging on our property? I heard the sound again—clearly someone was here. I cleared the potting shed, the direction I assumed the noise was coming from, but there was no one there. Just a shovel on the ground. An old rusty shovel and the beginnings of a hole.

"Who's out here? Come out now!" I yelled, ignoring my own goose bumps. Then I heard movement in the shed beside me. Yes, someone was hiding in there. I moved as quietly as possible toward the door and turned the knob slowly, hoping to get the drop on whoever might be inside. I was wasting my time—there was no one in here, no one at all, and no sign that there had been anyone in here recently.

Not at first, but then I saw them. Pink rose petals scattered around an empty bed of soil. Where had those come from? We hadn't had roses in at least two months. I realized the petals weren't just scattered...they spelled something. I studied them and after a few seconds could clearly read two words: *Thank you.* I reached into my pocket and retrieved my cell phone to take a picture. Jesse had to see this.

Before I could hit send, I saw a figure walk past the shed window. Instantly, I knew who it was.

That was John Jeffrey Belle! I raced to the door and yelled, "JB!" But he wasn't there, and the space where I was standing was icy cold. I spun around and called again, "JB! John Jeffrey Belle, I'm here!" But nothing happened. I didn't see him again, but I knew he had been there and had come back for one reason—to thank me. To thank us. And something else. The hole that I saw just a few moments ago was deeper now, and I spotted a rusty can peeking out from the soil. Quick as I could, I got on my knees and pried the can out of the clay.

"What is this, JB?" I whispered to the air around me but received no answer. And try as I might, I couldn't remove the lid. It was rusted on there. Feeling desperate, I whacked it against the rusty shovel, and the can released its long-hidden treasures.

I couldn't believe my eyes. Inside was a tangled assortment of oddities, including dry rotted ribbons, pieces of fabric and jewelry. Old jewelry. With shaking fingers, I plucked out a wad of silver and gasped at the diamonds that twinkled back at me. After a few seconds, I had the ribbons unwound and spread the elegant web of diamonds on my knee. "What in the world?" I kept pulling items out: an ivory brooch, a pair of ruby earrings, a thin gold cuff bracelet with a dangling pendant. I held the pendant up to the sunlight and could clearly see the initials MM. "Mariana? These were Mariana's?" And the rest of the contents were similar and familiar. Yes, I'd seen these before! These belonged to the McIntyre family. JB must have found them, and now he wanted us to have them.

I quickly put the lid back on and told myself, "I have to show Jesse." I packed everything back in the can and headed back to the house. I whispered, "Thank you, John Jeffrey Belle. Thank you all. Go be with your girls and Dot. She's waiting for you too. Kiss Marisol for me." As I left the potting shed behind, there were tears in my eyes. But I wasn't hurt or broken.

I was whole now.

And unlike Eddie, becoming whole wasn't about money or making someone hurt because I hurt. It was about family, loving family, staying together and keeping your promises. In some strange way, the Belles had been my family. Harper, Jeopardy, Addison and Loxley were all my sisters. I did for them what I couldn't do for myself, and that was bring everyone home.

But that wasn't true. Harper had brought me to Summerleigh. She'd entrusted it to me, and I had done what she could not, and I was glad that I could do it. Summerleigh, with all her shadows and mournful ghosts—all her secrets were revealed now. The Belles and McIntyres could rest knowing that there were no more secrets. That everyone was home and not forgotten.

Yes, it was time to let them rest. I got back to the house and climbed into my car with the can of treasures. With one last whispered, "Thank you," I turned off Hurlette and onto Highway 98. Time to look to the future. Of course, I wouldn't be gone long. Jesse said the book signing would only last a few hours. And then we'd come back home to Summerleigh.

And it would be just the two of us...until our little one joined us. We would fill Summerleigh with what it had been missing all these years. Laughter and love.

Read more from M.L. Bullock

The Seven Sisters Series

Seven Sisters
Moonlight Falls on Seven Sisters
Shadows Stir at Seven Sisters
The Stars that Fell
The Stars We Walked Upon
The Sun Rises Over Seven Sisters

The Idlewood Series

The Ghosts of Idlewood
Dreams of Idlewood
The Whispering Saint
The Haunted Child

Return to Seven Sisters
(A Sequel Series to Seven Sisters)

The Roses of Mobile
All the Summer Roses
Blooms Torn Asunder

The Gulf Coast Paranormal Series

The Ghosts of Kali Oka Road
The Ghosts of the Crescent Theater
A Haunting at Bloodgood Row
The Legend of the Ghost Queen
A Haunting at Dixie House
The Ghost Lights of Forrest Field
The Ghost of Gabrielle Bonet
The Ghost of Harrington Farm

Shabby Hearts Paranormal Cozy Mystery Series

A Touch of Shabby

To receive updates on her latest releases,
visit her website at MLBullock.com
and subscribe to her mailing list.
You can also contact her at
authormlbullock@gmail.com.

About the Author

Author of the best-selling *Seven Sisters* series and the *Desert Queen* series, M.L. Bullock has been storytelling since she was a child. A student of archaeology, she loves weaving stories that feature her favorite historical characters—including Nefertiti. She currently lives on the Gulf Coast with her family but travels frequently to explore the southern states she loves so much.

More from M.L. Bullock

From the *Ultimate Seven Sisters Collection*

A smile crept across my face when I turned back to look at the pale faces watching me from behind the lace curtains of the girls' dormitory. I didn't feel sorry for any of them—all of those girls hated me. They thought they were my betters because they were orphans and I was merely the accidental result of my wealthy mother's indiscretion. I couldn't understand why they felt that way. As I told Marie Bettencourt, at least my parents were alive and wealthy. Hers were dead and in the cold, cold ground. "Worm food now, I suppose." Her big dark eyes had swollen with tears, her ugly, fat face contorting as she cried. Mrs. Bedford scolded me for my remarks, but even that did not worry me.

I had a tool much more effective than Mrs. Bedford's threats of letters to the attorney who distributed my allowance or a day without a meal. Mr. Bedford would defend me—for a price. I would have to kiss his thin, dry lips and pretend that he did not peek at my décolletage a little too long. Once he even squeezed my bosom ever so quickly with his rough hands but then pretended it had been an accident. Mr. Bedford never had the courage to lift up my skirt or ask me for a "discreet favor," as my previous chaperone had called it, but I enjoyed making him stare. It had been great fun for a month or two until I saw how easily he could be manipulated.

And now my rescuer had come at last, a man, Louis Beaumont, who claimed to be my mother's brother. I had never met Olivia, my mother. Not that I could remember, anyway, and I assumed I never would.

Louis Beaumont towered above most men, as tall as an otherworldly prince. He had beautiful blond hair that I wanted to plunge my hands into. It looked like the down of a baby duckling. He had fair skin—so light it almost glowed—with pleasant features, even brows, thick lashes, a manly mouth. It was a shame he was so near a kin because I would have had no objections to whispering "Embrasse-moi" in his ear. Although I very much doubted Uncle Louis would have indulged my fantasy. How I loved to kiss, and to kiss one so beautiful! That would be heavenly. I had never kissed a handsome man before—I kissed the ice boy once and a farmhand, but neither of them had been handsome or good at kissing.

For three days we traveled in the coach, my uncle explaining what he wanted and how I would benefit if I followed his instructions. According to my uncle, Cousin Calpurnia needed me, or rather, needed a companion for the season. The heiress would come out this year, and a certain level of decorum was expected, including traveling with a suitable companion. "Who would be more suitable than her own cousin?" he asked me with the curl of a smile on his regal face. "Now, dearest Isla," he said, "I am counting on you to be a respectable girl. Leave all that happened before behind in Birmingham—no talking of the Bedfords or anyone else from that life. All will be well now." He patted my hand gently. "We must find Calpurnia a suitable husband, one that will give her the life she's accustomed to and deserves."

Yes, indeed. Now that this Calpurnia needed a proper companion, I had been summoned. I'd never even heard of Miss Calpurnia Cottonwood until now. Where had Uncle Louis been when I ran sobbing in a crumpled dress after falling prey to the lecherous hands of General Harper, my first guardian? Where had he been when I endured the shame and pain of my stolen maidenhead? Where? Was I not Beaumont stock and worthy of rescue? Apparently not. I decided then and there to hate my cousin, no matter how rich she was. Still, I smiled, spreading the skirt of my purple dress neatly around me on the seat. "Yes, Uncle Louis."

"And who knows, ma petite Cherie, perhaps we can find you a good match too. Perhaps a military man or a wealthy merchant. Would you like that?" I gave him another smile and nod before I pretended to be distracted by something out the window. My fate would be in my own hands, that much I knew. Never would I marry. I would make my own future. Calpurnia must be a pitiful, ridiculous kind of girl if she needed my help to land a "suitable" husband with all her affluence.

About the *Ultimate Seven Sisters Collection*

When historian Carrie Jo Jardine accepted her dream job as chief historian at Seven Sisters in Mobile, Alabama, she had no idea what she would encounter. The moldering old plantation housed more than a few boxes of antebellum artifacts and forgotten oil paintings. Secrets lived there—and they demanded to be set free.

This contains the entire supernatural suspense series.

More from M.L. Bullock

From *The Ghosts of Idlewood*

I arrived at Idlewood at seven o'clock thinking I'd have plenty of time to mark the doors with taped signs before the various contractors arrived. There was no electricity, so I wasn't sure what the workmen would actually accomplish today. I'd dressed down this morning in worn blue jeans and a long-sleeved t-shirt. It just felt like that kind of day. The house smelled stale, and it was cool but not freezing. We'd enjoyed a mild February this year, but like they say, "If you don't like the weather in Mobile, just wait a few minutes."

I really hated February. It was "the month of love," and this year I wasn't feeling much like celebrating. I'd given Chip the heave-ho for good right after Christmas, and our friendship hadn't survived the breakup. I hated that because I really did like him as a person, even if he could be narrow-minded about spiritual subjects. I hadn't been seeing anyone, but I was almost ready to get back into the dating game. Almost.

I changed out the batteries in my camera before beginning to document the house. Carrie Jo liked having before, during and after shots of every room.

According to the planning sheet Carrie Jo and I developed last month, all the stage one doors were marked. On her jobs, CJ orchestrated everything: what rooms got painted first, where the computers would go, which room we would store supplies in, that sort of thing. I also put no-entry signs on rooms that weren't safe or were off-limits to curious workers. The home was mostly empty, but there were some pricy mantelpieces and other components that would fetch a fair price if you knew where to unload stolen items such as high-end antiques. Surprisingly, many people did.

I'd start the pictures on the top floor and work my way down. I peeked out the front door quickly to see if CJ was here. No sign of her yet, which wasn't like her at all. She was usually the early bird. I smiled, feeling good that Carrie Jo trusted me enough to give me the keys to this grand old place. There were three floors, although the attic space wasn't a real priority for our project. The windows would be changed, the floors and roof inspected, but not a lot of cosmetic changes were planned for up there beyond that. We'd prepare it for future storage of seasonal decorations and miscellaneous supplies. Seemed a waste to me. I liked the attic; it was roomy, like an amazing loft apartment. But it was no surprise I was drawn to it—when I was a kid, I practically lived in my tree house.

I stuffed my cell phone in my pocket and jogged up the wide staircase in the foyer. I could hear birds chirping upstairs; they probably flew in through a broken window. There were quite a few of them from the sound of it. Since I hadn't labeled any doors upstairs or in the attic, I hadn't had the opportunity to explore much up there. It felt strangely exhilarating to do so all by myself. The first flight of stairs appeared safe, but I took my time on the next two. Water damage wasn't always easy to spot, and I had no desire to fall through a weak floor. When I reached the top of the stairs to the attic, I turned the knob and was surprised to find it locked.

"What?" I twisted it again and leaned against the door this time, but it wouldn't move. I didn't see a keyhole, so that meant it wasn't locked after all. I supposed it was merely stuck, the wood probably swollen from moisture. "Rats," I said. I set my jaw and tried one last time. The third time must have been the charm because it opened freely, as if it hadn't given me a world of problems before. I nearly fell as it gave way, laughing at myself as I regained my balance quickly. I reached for my camera and flipped it to the video setting. I panned the room to record the contents. There were quite a few old trunks, boxes and even the obligatory dressmaker's dummy. It was a nerd girl historian's dream come true.

Like an amateur documentarian, I spoke to the camera: "Maiden voyage into the attic at Idlewood. Today is February 4th. This is Rachel Kowalski recording."

Rachel Kowalski recording, something whispered back. My back straightened, and the fine hairs on my arms lifted as if to alert me to the presence of someone or something unseen.

I froze and said, "Hello?" I was happy to hear my voice and my voice alone echo back to me.

Hello?

About *The Ghosts of Idlewood*

When a team of historians takes on the task of restoring the Idlewood plantation to its former glory, they discover there's more to the moldering old home than meets the eye. The long-dead Ferguson children don't seem to know they're dead. A mysterious clock, a devilish fog and the Shadow Man add to the supernatural tension that begins to build in the house. Lead historian Carrie Jo Stuart and her assistant Rachel must use their special abilities to get to the bottom of the many mysteries that the house holds.

Detra Ann and Henri get a reality check, of the supernatural kind, and Deidre Jardine finally comes face to face with the past.

More from M.L. Bullock

From *The Ghosts of Kali Oka Road*

"Sierra to base."

Sara's well-manicured nails wrapped around the black walkie-talkie. "This is base. Go ahead, Sierra."

"Five minutes. No sign of the client. K2 is even Steven. Temp is 58F."

"Great. Check back in five. Radio silence, please."

"All right."

She tapped the antenna of the walkie-talkie to her chin. "I hope she remembers to take pictures. Did she take her camera?" she asked Midas. It was the first time she'd spoken to him this afternoon.

"Yes, but it wouldn't hurt to have a backup. You have yours?"

Sara cocked an eyebrow at him. "Are you kidding? I'm no rookie." She cast a stinging look of disdain in my direction and strolled back to her car in her stylish brown boots and began searching her back seat, presumably for her camera.

"Am I missing something?" I couldn't help but ask. The uncomfortable feeling kept rising. I'd had enough weirdness for one day.

Nobody answered me. Midas glared after Sara, but it was Peter who broke the silence.

"Cassidy, have you always been interested in the supernatural? Seems like we all have our own stories to tell. All of us have either seen something or lost someone. They say the loss of a loved one in a tragic way makes you more sensitive to the spirit world. I think that might be true."

"You're an ass, Pete. You're joking about her sister? She doesn't know she's lost her." I could see Midas' muscles ripple under his shirt. He wore a navy blue sweater, the thin, fitted kind that had three buttons at the top.

"I'm sorry, Cassidy. I swear to you I'm not a heartless beast."

"How could you not know?" Sara scolded him. "She told us about her the other night."

"I had my headphones on half the time, cueing up video and photographs. Shoot. I'm really sorry, Cassie."

That was the last straw. I was about to tell him how I really felt about his "joke." I took a deep breath and said, "My name is Cassidy, and..."

The walkie-talkie squawked, and I heard Sierra's voice, "Hey! Y'all need to get in here, now!"

Immediately everyone began running toward the narrow pathway. Midas snatched the walkie. "Sierra! What's up?"

"Someone's out here—stalking us."

"Can you see who it is? Is it Ranger?"

"Definitely not! Footsteps are too fast for someone so sick." Her whisper sent a shiver down my spine. "I'm taking pictures...should we keep pushing in toward the house?"

"Yes, keep going. We're double-timing your way. Stay on the path, Sierra. Don't get lost. Follow your GPS. It should lead you right to it."

"Okay."

"Midas! Let's flank whoever this is!" Pete said, his anger rising.

Midas looked at me as if to say, "Are you going to be all right?"

Sara said, "Go and help Sierra. Cassidy and I will follow."

Immediately Midas took off to the left and Peter to the right. They flanked the narrow road and scurried through the woods to see if they could detect the intruder.

Sara handed me her audio recorder. "Hold this! I'm grabbing some photos. We're going to run, Cassidy. I hope you can keep up."

"Sure, I used to run marathons." I didn't want to seem like a wimp. Now didn't seem like the time to tell her that I hadn't trained in over six months. "But why are we running? Are they in danger, do you think? Maybe it's just a homeless person."

"The element of surprise! Hit record and come on! Get your ass in gear, girl!"

I pressed the record button, gritted my teeth and took off after her. We ran down the leaf-littered path; the afternoon sunlight was casting lean shadows in a few spots now. We'd be out of sun soon. Then we'd be running through the woods in the dark. Was it supposed to be this cold out here?

I wish I held the temperature thingy instead, but I didn't.

"You feel that, Cassidy? The cold?" She bounded over a log in front of me, and I followed her. "Not unusual for the woods, but this is more than that," she said breathlessly. "I think it might mean we've got supernatural activity out here."

"You think?" I asked sincerely.

She paused her running. Her pretty cheeks were pink and healthy-looking. She'd worn her long hair in a ponytail today, and she wore blue jeans that fit her perfectly.

"Yeah, I do. I think it's time you get your feet wet, rookie. Use the audio recorder. Ask a few questions."

"Um, what? What kind of questions?"

"Ask a question like, 'Are there any spirits around me that want to talk?'"

I repeated what she said. I spun around slowly and looked around the forest, but there wasn't a sound.

Not even bird sounds or a squirrel rattling through the leaves. And it didn't just sound dead; it felt dead.

About *The Ghosts of Kali Oka Road*

The paranormal investigators at Gulf Coast Paranormal thought they knew what they were doing. Midas, Sierra, Sara, Josh and Peter had over twenty combined years of experience investigating supernatural activity on the Gulf Coast. But when they meet Cassidy, a young artist with a strange gift, they realize there's more to learn. And time is running out for Cassidy.

When Gulf Coast Paranormal begins investigating the ghosts of Kali Oka Road, they find an entity far scarier than a few ghosts. Add in the deserted Oak Grove Plantation, and you have a recipe for a night of terror.

More from M.L. Bullock

From *Wife of the Left Hand*

Okay, so it was official. I *had* lost my mind. I turned off the television and got up from the settee. I couldn't explain any of it, and who would believe me? Too many weird things had happened today— ever since I arrived at Sugar Hill.

Just walk away, Avery. Walk away. That had always been good advice, Vertie's advice, actually.

And I did.

I took a long hot bath, slid into some comfortable pinstriped pajamas, pulled my hair into a messy bun and climbed into my king-sized bed.

All was well. Until about midnight.

A shocking noise had me sitting up straight in the bed. It was the loudest, deepest clock I had ever heard, and it took forever for the bells to ring twelve times. After the last ring, I flopped back on my bed and pulled the covers over my head. Would I be able to go back to sleep now?

To my surprise, the clock struck once more. What kind of clock struck thirteen? Immediately my room got cold, the kind of cold that would ice you down to your bones. Wrapping the down comforter around me, I turned on the lamp beside me and huddled in the bed, waiting...for something...

I sat waiting, wishing I were brave enough and warm enough to go relight a fire in my fireplace. It was so cold I could see my breath now. Thank God I hadn't slept nude tonight. Jonah had hated when I wore pajamas to bed. *Screw him!* I willed myself to stop thinking about him. That was all in the past now. He'd made his choice, and I had made mine.

Then I heard the sound for the first time. It was soft at first, like a kitten crying pitifully. Was there a lost cat here? That would be totally possible in this big old house. As the mewing sound drew closer, I could hear much more clearly it was not a kitten but a child. A little girl crying as if her heart were broken. Sliding my feet in my fuzzy white slippers and wrapping the blanket around me tightly, I awkwardly tiptoed to the door to listen. Must be one of the housekeepers' children. Probably cold and lost. I imagined if you wanted to, you could get lost here and never be found. Now her crying mixed with whispers as if she were saying something; she was pleading as if her life depended on it. My heart broke at the sound, but I couldn't bring myself to open the door and actually take a look. Not yet. I scrambled for my iPhone and jogged back to the door to record the sounds. How else would anyone believe me? Too many unbelievable things had happened today. With my phone in one hand, the edge of my blanket in my teeth to keep it in place and my free hand on the doorknob, I readied myself to open the door. I had to see who—or what—was crying in the hallway. I tried to turn the icy cold silver-toned knob, but it wouldn't budge. It was as if someone had locked me in. Who would do such a thing? Surely not Dinah or Edith or one of the other staff?

About *Wife of the Left Hand*

Avery Dufresne had the perfect life: a rock star boyfriend, a high-profile career in the anchor chair on a national news program. Until a serious threat brings her perfect world to a shattering stop. When Avery emerges from the darkness she finds she has a new ability—a supernatural one. Avery returns to Belle Fontaine, Alabama, to claim an inheritance: an old plantation called Sugar Hill. Little does she know that the danger has just begun.

More from M.L. Bullock

From *A Touch of Shabby*

I wolfed down the sandwich, sipped on the soup and then lay on the couch to catch forty winks. I had every intention of getting a shower before passing out, but I was so tired now. I'd been up since 5 o'clock this morning as I always tried to be. Yep, I was an early bird and came from a long line of early birds, which meant I preferred early to bed too.

That was something Armand used to hate. He liked closing the bars around Lake Dennis every weekend. We were just too different. At first, he'd been kind of wild and exciting, but as I got to know him, I realized his behavior was less wild and exciting and more childish and dangerous. *And why am I thinking about him?* I asked myself once again.

Oh yeah. Because I'm lonely.

I'd gotten a lot accomplished today after the tow truck debacle, including cleaning out Trailer Four and putting a fresh coat of paint in its laundry room. Thankfully, the family who lived there were tidy folks, so it was a light job. But who thought an eggplant purple paint job was a good idea? It had taken me three coats to cover up the horrible shade, but the laundry room didn't make me want to tear my hair out now.

Sometimes Tiffany helped out with the light maintenance, but she'd been busy shuttling cats to the vet recently when she wasn't picking up extra shifts at the restaurant. Luckily for her, one of the waitresses was having a baby...her third, and she was only twenty-five. Tiffany had spent a small fortune on spaying and neutering over the past six months, so I knew she could use the extra money.

With thoughts of feral cats and rented trailers running through my mind, I fell asleep and slept hard for quite a while. I woke up to a dark trailer. My television was off; as I'd learned from frequent practice, it clicked off after three hours. But there was no reason why the rest of the place should be dark. Even the sink light wasn't on, and I left that on perpetually.

Shoot, the power must be out.

I reached for my cell phone and discovered it had died too. That was weird. I had a charged battery earlier, didn't I? Walking carefully to the kitchen, I dug around in the tool drawer to retrieve my LED flashlight. That's when I heard footsteps across my front porch. Heavy, clumsy footsteps. And then down they went. My heart leaped in my chest as I listened intently. Was someone trying to break in here? The sound of my trash cans banging around put those worries to rest. Obviously, this was an animal looking for a quick meal. The metal trash can lids clanged on the ground. *Must be raccoons in the garbage.* I shut the flashlight off and peered out the window. The whole darn trailer park was dark; there wasn't a light on, except at the end of the street. Duval's generator must have kicked on because his house was lit up like a Cajun Christmas tree. The weather was calm; there wasn't a storm in sight. So what had caused this outage? Someone must have hit a power pole.

I heard the crashing sound again, and this time, a growl accompanied the clattering. *That's no raccoon*, I thought. I narrowed my eyes and strained to see in the dark.

Yeah, definitely not a raccoon. It's too big to be a... What the heck is that?

For the life of me, I couldn't figure it out. I flicked on the flashlight and shot a beam of light in the direction of my toppled trash cans. To my complete shock, a big hairy figure rose up and poked its head out at me as if it wanted to get a closer look. *Oh no! It can see me!* I swore like a sailor and stepped back to hide behind the curtain, flattening my body against the wall. My heart pounded in my chest like an iron drum as I talked myself down from completely freaking out. I scooted down to the ground and forced myself to breathe normally.

"There's a perfectly good explanation for this. Just keep calm and remember you're the boss."

I got back up, turned my flashlight back on and focused the beam in the creature's direction. The thing was gone now, but my trash was torn to shreds. I breathed a sigh of relief and annoyance.

Great. And tomorrow is garbage day.

Despite my aggravation at having my garbage destroyed, I didn't venture outside to check it out further. The garbage could wait until the sun came up. I sat on the couch, my hands trembling and my mouth dry. What should I do now? Call 911? Or Gus, maybe?

I couldn't believe it, but for the first time in my life, I'd seen what I'd never expected to see.

I was pretty sure I'd just seen Bigfoot.

About *A Touch of Shabby*

Arcadia Shabeaux can't believe her luck.

Aunt Mavis hands her the keys to the family business, the Shabby Hearts Trailer Park and Campground, but there's a catch. It's only two weeks before tourist season begins and the place is in major disrepair. Lake Dennis isn't the hottest spot on the "Redneck Riviera," but Arcadia has plans to change all that. That is, if she can keep her dysfunctional family, a nosy Bigfoot and an overbearing television reporter in check. Add to the madness Arcadia's arrogant ex-boyfriend and an attractive newcomer who's caught her eye, and you've got a sure-fire recipe for disaster--and fun!

When Pierre Ledbetter, the owner of the Happy Hooker Bait Shop, disappears, the residents of Shabby Hearts naturally blame it on the legendary cryptid. Everyone except the sheriff, who believes a Shabeaux has to be responsible. The tension rises when a resident of the trailer park dies mysteriously and the Lake Dennis community erupts into chaos. Arcadia isn't sure how it will all play out, but she is determined to uncover the truth as quickly as possible.

Immerse yourself in a humorous, small-town trailer park cozy mystery with a side order of the paranormal.

CPSIA information can be obtained
at www.ICGtesting.com
Printed in the USA
BVHW041149170519
548614BV00010B/103/P